TEEN BOYS ON C...
Recent Rash of Robberies Baffle Bayport Police

(*Bayport County News*)

Several small convenience stores were robbed this past week in the Bayport area. Witnesses describe the culprits as a pair of teenage boys wearing windbreakers with hoods. "One was blond and the other had dark hair," said Dolly Crumb, the owner of Dolly's Deli on Longview Drive. "They were nice-looking boys too. But they didn't act very nice. They made me lie on the floor while they made their getaway." Other businesses targeted by the teen robbers include Blue Jay's Mini-Mart, Burger Bob's, and Grocer's Corner. Bayport police have no leads as to the identities of the two boys but are asking local business owners to be on the lookout. If you have any information on the crimes, please contact the nearest police station.

THE HARDY BOYS

UNDERCOVER BROTHERS™

Available from Simon & Schuster

THE HARDY BOYS

UNDERCOVER BROTHERS™

Super Mystery

#1 Wanted

FRANKLIN W. DIXON

Aladdin Paperbacks

New York   London   Toronto   Sydney

This book is a work of fiction. Any references to historical events, real people, or real locales are used fictitiously. Other names, characters, places, and incidents are the product of the author's imagination, and any resemblance to actual events or locales or persons, living or dead, is entirely coincidental.

👣 ALADDIN PAPERBACKS
An imprint of Simon & Schuster
Children's Publishing Division
1230 Avenue of the Americas
New York, NY 10020

Copyright © 2006 by Simon & Schuster, Inc.

THE HARDY BOYS MYSTERY STORIES and HARDY BOYS UNDER-COVER BROTHERS are trademarks of Simon & Schuster, Inc.
ALADDIN PAPERBACKS and colophon are trademarks of Simon & Schuster, Inc.
Designed by Lisa Vega
The text of this book was set in Aldine 401BT.
Manufactured in the United States of America
First Aladdin Paperbacks edition June 2006
20 19 18 17 16 15 14 13 12 11

Library of Congress Control Number 2005929519
ISBN-13: 978-1-4169-1258-3
ISBN-10: 1-4169-1258-4
1113 OFF

TABLE OF CONTENTS

Prologue

It was the perfect day for a bank robbery.

The weatherman had predicted rain, and for once he was right. The sky was filled with dark gray storm clouds. A rumble of thunder shook the ground, and a sudden downpour drove everyone from the streets.

That meant fewer witnesses.

Perfect.

Two boys stood on the sidewalk in the rain, watching and waiting.

The younger blond teenager yawned. "Why are we doing this so early? I'm still half-asleep."

His dark-haired brother sighed. "Because people cash their paychecks every Friday at lunch hour. So the tellers fill their drawers with extra money in the morning."

"How do you know?"

"I'm the smart one, remember?"

"Yeah, right." The blond boy rubbed his eyes. "I just want to go back to bed."

"Well, too bad. We've been planning this for weeks. You can't wimp out now."

The boys turned and gazed through the huge

plateglass window of the bank. It was almost empty inside—except for a couple of older ladies waiting in line.

"Now's our chance," said the older boy. "Let's go."

They pulled the hoods of their windbreakers over their heads and entered the front door of the bank. An overweight bank guard leaned back in a chair, snoring loudly.

The two boys ignored him and marched straight to the front of the bank line.

"Excuse me, young man," said one of the older women in line. "We were waiting here first."

"Get over it, Grandma. We're in a hurry," the younger boy snapped back.

The teller behind the window looked up at the two boys. She had curly red hair, thick glasses—and a puzzled look on her face. "Um, could I help you boys?" she asked.

The dark-haired teen reached into his pocket and pulled out a note. Quickly unfolding it, he slipped it beneath the glass window.

The teller glanced down to read the message. "Oh, my," she muttered. Her mouth dropped open, and her eyes nearly popped out of her head.

The boys expected a reaction like this.

The note read: "Empty your cash drawer into a bag and no one will get hurt."

The older boy leaned toward the window and lowered his voice. "Don't even think about pushing the alarm button, either."

The teller bit her lip and started trembling.

"Don't mess it up, lady," the younger boy added. "Just give us the money."

The red-haired woman nodded nervously and opened her cash drawer. With shaky hands, she began stuffing wads of cash into a zippered bag.

"That's it," said the older boy. "Just fill up the bag. And don't try anything funny."

The teller emptied her entire cash drawer into the bag, then zipped it up.

"Now slide it under the window," said the younger boy.

The woman took a deep breath and pushed the bag through the slot. The older boy grabbed it and smiled. "Thanks, ma'am," he said. "It was nice doing business with you."

The two boys turned and started walking toward the exit of the bank.

That's when the red-haired teller pushed the alarm button.

RRRRINNNNG!

The sleeping guard almost fell out of his chair. He rubbed his eyes and looked up.

"Stop those boys!" the teller shrieked. "They just robbed the bank!"

The security guard reached for his gun.

"Freeze!" the older boy shouted. "Get down on the floor or we'll blow the place up!"

"Yeah! Get down!" said the younger boy. "We're wired with explosives!"

The guard dropped his arm away from his gun. Slowly he lowered himself down on the floor. The two older women in line gasped.

"You too, ladies!" the older boy yelled. "Get down!"

The women squealed and squatted down, covering their faces.

"Don't move until we're gone," said the younger boy. "Start counting to five hundred."

The guard and the women started counting.

The older boy looked at his partner. "Come on," he said. "Let's get out of here, Joe."

"I'm right behind you, Frank."

The two boys ran out of the bank and into the rain.

1.

"Eat Sand!"

"I *knew* we'd get caught," I said to Frank.

My brother didn't say anything. He just glared at me and struggled against the ropes tied around his hands and feet.

"Those beach bums suspected us from the start," I went on. "They knew we were asking too many questions."

Frank ignored me. Flopping onto his side, he tried twisting himself free, but the ropes only seemed to tighten even more.

"You're making it worse, Frank."

"You're driving me crazy, Joe."

I was about to make a suggestion when I heard something in the distance.

It was the sound of dirt bikes.

Frank stopped struggling. "Listen," he said. "They're coming this way. We can yell for help."

5

"They'll never hear us, Frank."

My brother shot me a dirty look and wriggled on the sandy ground toward the bike trail. A few seconds later, the dirt bikes came closer and closer—their motors growing louder and louder.

"Help!" Frank shouted. "Help us! Help!"

The dirt bikes zipped past us without even stopping.

I glanced at Frank and smirked.

"Don't say it," he mumbled.

I couldn't resist. "I told you so."

"I said don't say it."

I started to laugh.

"I don't know why you think this is so funny," said Frank. "You're tied up too."

"Yes, but I have a pocketknife in my boot," I explained.

Frank sighed. "Why didn't you say so? And why aren't you cutting us free?"

I arched my back and slowly pulled the knife from my boot. "I'm working on it," I said, struggling against the rope around my wrists. "There. I got it."

I opened the knife behind my back and carefully started cutting through the rope. In a few minutes, my hands were free. Then I untied the rope around my feet.

"Well?" said Frank. "Are you going to cut me loose?"

"I'm thinking about it."

"Well, what are you waiting for?"

"I'm waiting for you to admit that you blew our cover by asking too many questions."

"Sure, whatever," said Frank, gasping. "Just cut me loose."

I bent over and cut through my brother's ropes. As soon as he was free, Frank stood up and started walking toward the bike trail.

"Where are you going?" I asked.

"To park headquarters," he answered. "To report the thieves."

Maybe I should explain.

Frank and I are undercover agents for ATAC— American Teens Against Crime. Our latest mission involved a pair of beach-bum thieves who were stealing dirt bikes and dune buggies from the Off-Road Vehicle Park on the Jersey Shore. It was a pretty cool assignment. You could rent all sorts of vehicles by the hour and spend the day racing through the park's giant maze of trails, jumps, and sand dunes. The first day we were here, Frank and I spotted the culprits—a shady-looking pair of long-haired dudes with bandannas who always seemed to be lurking in the background.

I told Frank to lie low for a few days. But my brother couldn't resist asking the suspects questions: "How often do you guys come here? What are the best trails? Which dirt bikes are the fastest?"

A few hours later the bandanna dudes jumped us,

tied us up, and dumped us along one of the bike trails in the woods.

"Good thing I had my pocketknife," I said as we walked toward the park headquarters.

"Okay, you're a hero, Joe," my brother answered. "Now drop it, okay?"

I chuckled to myself. Frank hated it when I was right.

We reached the main entrance a few minutes later. Walking past row after row of rental bikes, we headed toward the concrete headquarters near the gate. As soon as we stepped through the doorway, a shortwave radio buzzed behind the desk.

A tall park ranger with a mustache picked up the speaker. "What's up?"

A voice crackled through the radio. "We have a dune buggy theft in progress! Vehicle stolen on the main beach!"

Frank grabbed my arm. "Come on!"

We turned and ran from the building.

"We'll never catch them on foot," I said.

"I know," he said.

Dashing across the sidewalk, Frank leaped on one of the rental dirt bikes and revved up the engine. I hopped on the bike next to his. "Hey!" shouted the park ranger, running after us. "You boys didn't pay for those! Wait!"

Frank threw the park ranger a few bills. "Here you go," he said. "Keep the change—for the park."

What a Boy Scout!

We tore off on the dirt bikes, kicking up sand and roaring down the nearest trail.

"Where's the main beach?" I shouted at Frank.

He nodded at a sign at the fork of the road. The beach was to the right. Tilting our bikes, we zoomed down the trail toward the sandy dunes.

I glanced behind me to see if anyone was following us.

Nope. Dead quiet. Then—

"Joe! Look out!"

I spun my head around. A pair of bikers were heading straight for me.

"Whoa!"

Turning sharply, I swerved around the oncoming bikes and careened off a dune. My front tire flew into the air, and then the whole bike bounced back onto the trail.

Frank skidded and spun his bike around. "You okay, bro?"

"Totally," I shouted, zooming past him toward the beach.

"Hey! Wait up!"

Frank revved his engine and sped up behind me. A minute later we hit the main beach, our tires spinning in the dry sand. We pulled to a stop and looked around.

"Joe! Over there!"

My brother pointed across the beach toward a lime

green dune buggy. Even from a distance, I was able to recognize the bandanna dudes.

They were hooting and cheering—and getting away as fast as they could.

"After them!" Frank yelled.

We gunned our engines and tried to take off—but our wheels spun around in place, kicking sand in the air.

"These bikes are useless on the beach," I said.

Frank nudged my shoulder and pointed to the ocean. An empty dune buggy was parked near the shore. The driver had hopped out to wade in the waves.

"Come on," Frank whispered, hopping off his bike.

I followed him down the beach, ducking down as we approached the dune buggy. The driver didn't even notice as we jumped into the front seat.

I grabbed the wheel and turned the ignition key. The dune buggy roared to life—and the driver spun around.

"Hey! Wait! That's my buggy!"

"We're just borrowing it!" Frank yelled at the guy.

I slammed down on the gas, and the dune buggy shot across the beach. Frank pointed toward the dunes. I turned the wheel and headed after the lime green buggy. The bandanna dudes were getting away!

"Faster, Joe!"

I gave it the gas. The buggy zoomed up a huge sloping dune and soared through the air.

KA-THUMP!

We landed with a thud and bounced across the sand. I pulled hard on the wheel to keep from flipping over. I managed to steady the vehicle when—*wham*—we hit another dune, flying up, up, and down again. Dune after dune, we sped after the stolen buggy, moving closer and closer.

"We're gaining on them!" Frank shouted.

I cut around a small dune as fast as I could. The whole buggy tilted and bounced, both wheels on the right side rising up in the air.

"Hold on!" I yelled.

WHUMP!

The vehicle slammed down, digging into the sand and gaining speed. Seconds later we were pulling up next to the lime green buggy.

One bandanna dude turned his head and saw me.

"Hey, punk!" he sneered. "Eat dust!"

Then he slammed down on the brakes, turned his wheel hard, and spun away.

SWOOSH!

A blast of hot sand flew into our faces.

For a second I was blinded. I stopped the buggy and wiped the sand from my eyes.

"They're getting away!" Frank said, spitting up sand. "Hurry!"

I repositioned the vehicle and took off after them. Zooming up and down the dunes, we closed in on that green buggy until we were fifty feet behind it.

One of the buggy thieves turned around.

"That's right, buddy!" I snarled. "I'm right behind you!"

The dude smacked his pal on the shoulder and shouted into his ear. Then, without warning, the buggy spun around in the sand, skidding to a stop.

"What are they doing?" asked Frank.

I slammed on the brakes. Our buggies sat on opposite dunes, facing each other like prizefighters in a ring. Nobody moved. The thieves just sat there, grinning ear to ear, revving their engine.

"They want to play chicken, Frank," I said. "Fasten your seat belt."

My brother looked worried. "Are you sure you want to do this, Joe? We could get ourselves killed."

"Aw, come on. It'll be fun."

I shifted into neutral and revved the engine as loud as I could. The bandanna dudes responded with an even louder roar.

"Besides," I continued, "it doesn't seem to me like these guys are going to give up without a fight. This is our chance to stop them."

The sun blazed overhead. I held my breath—and waited for my opponents to make their move.

"Don't lose your cool, Joe."

"Don't be a backseat driver, Frank. I got it."

The lime green buggy purred softly. Then, with a sudden roar, it zoomed down the dune straight toward us.

"Go, Joe! Go!"

My brother braced himself as I shifted the gear and slammed the pedal to the metal.

Vrrrooom!

Sand flew in the air behind us. Our buggy shot forward with a jolt. Faster and faster we flew down the side of the dune—heading straight for the approaching vehicle.

"Watch out!" Frank shouted. "We're going to crash!"

"No, *they're* going to crash!" I yelled back.

I wasn't about to let those beach-bum thieves beat me. Hunching down, I gripped the wheel and floored it.

The bandanna dudes didn't swerve or flinch. They just kept on coming.

"They're not giving up, Joe!" my brother shouted.

"Neither am I!"

Forty feet, thirty feet, twenty feet—closer and closer we hurtled toward each other.

"Turn away, Joe!"

"No!"

"But—"

"No!"

Ten feet, five feet . . .

WHOOMP!

The dudes turned their wheel at the last second. Their buggy swerved away and scraped against our front tires.

CRUNCH!

Both buggies spun out of control, flying and flipping, up, up, and over.

"Hold on!" I yelled, bouncing with the buggy.

We tumbled upside down across the sand. Then we flipped over again, rolling and rolling, up and over, up and over. The sky and the sand spun around us so fast, I had no idea which way was up.

Good thing the buggy had a roll bar.

Otherwise we would have been flattened for sure.

KALOOOMP!

Finally the buggy bounced to a stop—faceup.

"Joe! Look!"

I rubbed the sand from my eyes to see where my brother was pointing. Fifteen feet away, the lime green buggy was upside down in a dune. Its wheels were spinning in the air.

The bandanna dudes were trapped!

"We got them," said Frank. "They're not going anywhere now."

"Except to jail," I added.

Suddenly we saw a couple of park rangers running across the dunes.

"Hey! Boys! Don't move!" one of them yelled.

"Come on," said Frank. "Let's get out of here."

We unbuckled our seat belts and hopped out of the buggy. Then we made a dash for the woods on the edge of the beach.

"Wait! Come back here!" shouted one of the rangers.

Frank and I weren't about to stop. We were undercover agents, after all, on a secret mission. So we quickly made our getaway while the rangers apprehended the thieves.

"This way!" said Frank. "We hid our motorcycles over here."

"No, Frank. We hid them over there. Look."

I pointed to our motorcycles behind a bunch of shrubs. Frank sighed and followed after me.

"I told you so," I said.

Frank growled.

He hates it when I'm right.

2.

The Dirt on Frank and Joe

My brother Joe was pretty proud of himself.

In a single day he had managed to cut through our ropes with a pocketknife, roll over a few times in a dune buggy, stop a pair of wanted criminals, and locate our hidden motorcycles.

Okay, fine.

But did he have to rub my nose in it?

"Who's the man, Frank?" he asked, when we stopped our motorcycles at a red light.

I rolled my eyes. "You're the man, Joe," I said. "Now will you cut it out? We're almost home."

The light changed, and we rode our motorcycles through downtown Bayport. When we reached the end of Main Street, I noticed a bunch of police cars in front of the local bank. One of the officers was questioning a woman with red hair and glasses.

Joe turned and looked at me.

I shrugged my shoulders and kept driving.

As we passed by, the red-haired woman stopped talking. She adjusted her glasses and stared at us. The police officer turned and stared too.

What are they looking at? I had a funny feeling in my gut. For a second, I understood what it must be like to stand in a suspect line at the police station.

Weird.

Joe and I leaned forward on our motorcycles and headed for home. By the time we pulled into the driveway, it was almost three in the afternoon. Not bad. We had made excellent time.

But Mom and Aunt Trudy seemed to think differently.

"*Now* you show up," said Aunt Trudy, "when we're almost finished with the yard work. Mmm-hmm."

She and Mom leaned on their garden rakes and looked at us.

"While you boys were hanging out at the mall, we've been slaving away," said Mom. "What's up? You promised you would be back in time to help us."

"Sorry, Mom. My watch needs a new battery." I hopped off my motorcycle and glanced at Dad, who had just finished mowing the lawn. He turned off the engine and winked at Joe and me.

"How'd it go, boys?" he asked under his breath.

"Everything's cool, Dad," I whispered.

"Thanks to me," Joe threw in.

I sighed. "That's right. Joe's the man."

Dad smiled and nodded.

Our father's a retired cop who knows all about our undercover missions. In fact, he was the creator of American Teens Against Crime. It's our little secret. Mom and Aunt Trudy have no idea that Joe and I are out hunting down criminals every chance we get. Dad thinks it's best if we don't worry them.

"There's still a lot of raking to do!" Aunt Trudy shouted across the front lawn.

I turned around. "No problem, Aunt Trudy. You and Mom go inside and rest. Joe and I will finish up here."

Joe slapped my arm.

"Thanks, boys," said Mom, dropping her rake. "The garbage bags are there on the porch step. Just bag the grass and stuff it all in the garbage cans behind the garage."

Aunt Trudy handed Joe a rake. "Here you go. I'll make you a pitcher of lemonade. It's hot out here."

"Thanks, Aunt Trudy."

Dad, Mom, and Aunt Trudy went inside, leaving Joe and me with a pair of rakes, a box of garbage bags, and a whole lawn full of freshly cut grass.

Joe looked at me and groaned.

"What a life," he said. "Undercover work in the morning, yard work in the afternoon."

I grabbed a rake. "Don't sweat it, Joe," I said. "You're the man."

Joe grumbled and started raking away.

There wasn't too much left to do. Mom and Aunt Trudy had already raked half the grass into neat piles across the lawn. But there was enough work to give me time to think.

"What's up, Frank?" Joe asked.

"What do you mean?"

"You have this look on your face," he said. "Kinda like how Trudy looks when Playback poops on her shoulder." (Playback's our pet parrot.)

I stopped raking and sighed.

"I was thinking about what we did at the park this morning," I told him. "I'm feeling a little guilty that we took that dune buggy."

"We didn't steal it. We left it at the park."

"I know," I explained. "But we should have paid a fee or something."

Joe shook his head. "We were trying to catch criminals, Frank."

"Yeah, but does that give us the right to *act* like criminals?"

I stared down at the ground, lost in my thoughts.

Joe threw a handful of grass in my face.

"Hey!"

I tackled him to the ground. Joe stumbled backward and landed with a thud on a soft pile of grass. I rolled on top of him, throwing handfuls of grass in his face.

"Payback!" I shouted.

Of course, that just made Joe fight back harder. Locked together, legs kicking, we rolled over and over across the lawn. Grass flew in the air around us.

"You're just making more work for yourselves, you know."

We stopped wrestling and looked up to see Aunt Trudy on the porch with a pitcher of lemonade.

"Uh . . . thanks for the lemonade, Aunt Trudy," I said, smiling.

She shook her head. "I don't know why I bother," she said. "You boys are nothing but troublemakers."

She set the pitcher down on the porch railing and went inside. I glanced at Joe—who threw another handful of grass in my face.

"You rat!"

We wrestled across the lawn, knocking over more of the neat piles of grass. Finally I managed to pin Joe to the ground.

"Okay, bro," I said, huffing and puffing. "Say Frank is the man."

"No way!"

"Say it! Frank is the man!"

Joe struggled beneath me. "No!"

"Say it!"

I started tickling him.

"Okay! Okay! Frank is the man! Frank is the man!"

I rolled off of Joe, laughing my head off. I shouldn't

have been surprised when he hit me with another handful of grass.

"You are so *not* the man, Frank!" he yelled.

I was about to tackle him again when Dad came out on the front porch. "Okay, knock it off," he said. "Tell me about your mission this morning."

Joe and I stopped fighting and walked toward the porch. First we poured ourselves some lemonade. Then we told him all about the bandanna dudes and the dune buggy chase.

Dad had a hard time hiding his smile. "So you just stole that poor guy's dune buggy while he was wading in the ocean?"

I felt a twinge of guilt.

"The thieves were getting away," Joe explained.

Dad let out a little laugh and shook his head.

"We took the dune buggy to catch the criminals," I said. "Is that stealing?"

Our father leaned back on the railing and rubbed his chin. "That's a tricky question," he answered. "Sometimes police officers have to bend the law to uphold the law. But you should never *break* the law unless it's absolutely necessary."

"So taking the dune buggy was wrong?"

Dad wrinkled his forehead. "I suppose so. But you were trying to help the park, not steal from it. In this case, I think the end justify the means."

That made me feel better.

"But you have to be careful," Dad continued. "Sometimes law enforcers can be corrupted by their own power. Sometimes good cops turn bad."

A shadow crossed over our father's face.

I glanced at Joe. "Well, I guess we'd better finish raking the lawn . . . or else Aunt Trudy will revoke our lemonade rights."

Dad tried to smile, but he still had that strange, haunted look on his face. Slowly he stood up and went inside the house.

"What was that all about?" Joe asked.

"I don't know," I answered, picking up a rake. "Maybe Dad has a dark past he's not telling us about."

Joe winced. "Dad? No way!"

I handed Joe a rake. "Come on. Start raking."

An hour later we had bagged all the grass. Joe and I each grabbed a couple of bags and started dragging them behind the garage. My brother reached down to pull the lid off of one of the metal cans.

"Um, Frank. Take a look at this."

I stepped next to Joe and looked into the can.

There was a medium-size package lying at the bottom. It was wrapped in plain brown paper and labeled in red ink.

It read: THE DIRT ON FRANK AND JOE.

I looked up at Joe.

"Another mission, Frank?" he asked.

"Either that, or Aunt Trudy is the world's most organized housekeeper."

Joe laughed and reached down for the package. "Let's go and check it out."

We leaned the rakes against the garage, went inside the house, and sneaked upstairs before anyone could see us. Once we were in my bedroom, I closed the door and turned on my computer.

"Poop."

"What, Frank?"

"There's parrot poop all over my desk."

Joe laughed and reached up to stroke Playback, who sat on his perch just a few feet away.

"Playback!" Joe cooed. "Have you been a bad boy?"

Playback squawked back.

"Bad boy! Bad boy! Bad boy!"

While Joe stroked the parrot's feathered chest, I opened up the package. The first thing I saw was a folded newspaper on top.

There was a large black-and-white photo of two boys standing inside a bank. The image was grainy and blurry. It looked like it had been taken with one of those security cameras.

And it definitely looked like a bank robbery in progress.

But that's not what shocked me.

What shocked me was that the robbers looked exactly like Joe and me.

"What is it, Frank?"

I took a deep breath. "We're in serious trouble, bro," I told him.

Playback squawked.

"Bad boys! Bad boys!"

LOCAL BANK ROBBED!
Teen Thieves "Graduate" to Federal Crime

(*Bayport County News*) At eleven o'clock this morning, the Bayport Bank on Main Street was robbed by a pair of teenage boys. According to eyewitness descriptions of the suspects, the boys appear to be the same criminals responsible for a recent series of convenience store thefts in the Bayport area. "The younger boy was blond, and the older one was dark-haired," said Rose Adams, the bank teller who emptied her cash drawer for the thieves. "They told us they were wired with explosives." Shaken by the robbery, Ms. Adams informed local police that she overheard the culprits call each other by name. If you know any teenage boys who fit this description, or who go by the names "Frank" and "Joe," please contact the nearest police station. Warning: The suspects may be armed and should be considered extremely dangerous.

3.
Wanted

I couldn't believe my eyes.

Two teenagers named *Frank* and *Joe*? *Wanted for bank robbery*?

"What's going on, Frank?" I asked.

My brother shook his head. "I have no idea. For a second, I thought we were in trouble for stealing that dune buggy."

I scoffed. "That doesn't seem so bad now, does it?"

"Compared to bank robbery? No."

I reached for the mission box. "What else is in here?"

Frank pulled out a few more newspaper clippings and started reading them. "They're articles about the convenience store robberies. All of them happened here in the Bayport area. And they were all committed by two boys who look exactly like us."

"Great."

"Now it's been reported that their names are Frank and Joe," said my brother, putting down the clippings. "You know what this means, don't you?"

"The cops are going to come after us."

"Exactly. I wouldn't be surprised if they're on their way here right now."

"I guess we'd better hurry, then," I said, digging deeper into the mission box.

Inside were two pairs of night-vision goggles, a set of high-powered binoculars, and a small electronic gadget with a screen and keyboard.

"What's this?" I asked.

Frank took the palm-size device and studied it. "Oh, it's one of those wireless pocket communicators," he explained. "We can retrieve phone messages with it and send or receive e-mails no matter where we are."

"Even if we're running from the law?" I asked.

Frank smirked. "Relax, Joe. We don't even know what's going on yet. Is there a mission CD in the box?"

I looked inside. A homemade CD lay on the bottom. "Yeah, here," I said, handing it to Frank.

My brother read the label. "Wanted."

I sighed. "It doesn't sound good. Pop it in, Frank. Let's see how much trouble we're in this time."

My brother slid the disc into his computer and clicked play. A second or two later the screen went black.

"They go by the names Frank and Joe," a deep voice boomed over the speakers.

Newspaper headlines flashed across the screen, followed by grainy black-and-white photos of two teenage boys.

"And they're Wanted,*"* said the voice.

The images froze. A pair of picture frames slammed down over two blurred head shots of the boys. There was a loud *clank* that sounded like a prison door slamming.

The word WANTED appeared in large block letters above the framed portraits.

"No one knows their real identities," the voice continued. *"They look like Hardys. They sound like Hardys. But they're doing things the Hardys would* never *do."*

The pictures faded. A neatly typed police bulletin rolled across the screen: a long list of local crimes.

"Frank and Joe are Wanted *for the following convenience store holdups: Blue Jay's Mini-Mart, May twenty-fifth. Burger Bob's, May thirtieth. Grocer's Corner, June fifth. Dolly's Deli, June ninth."*

"Wow, we've been busy," I muttered.

Frank slapped my arm and turned back to the screen.

"The boys are also suspected of several other crimes that, at this time, cannot be proven," said the voice on the speaker.

A motorcycle repair garage appeared on the screen.

I recognized it immediately. "Hey! That's Mickey's place on the highway!"

Frank shushed me.

"Two motorcycles vanished last month from Mickey's parking lot," the voice explained. *"We believe the thieves stole them so they could impersonate you."*

"Great," I said. "They have motorcycles, too."

The screen turned black again. Then a video image appeared. It looked like footage from one of the local TV stations. The camera was pointed at Bayport Bank on Main Street. A crowd of police officers surrounded several witnesses.

I recognized the red-haired lady from this morning.

"Look, Frank. There's the woman who kept staring at us when we drove down Main Street."

Frank nodded. "Now we know why. She thought we were the robbers, revisiting the scene of the crime."

The voice on the speakers described the bank robbery in detail. *"There were four witnesses: two older women waiting in line at the bank, the teller herself, and a bank guard who seemed to be sleeping through most of the robbery."*

"At least he won't describe us to the cops," I said.

A second later the guard proved me wrong. *"I think they used motorcycles for their getaway,"* he told a reporter. *"I heard a pair of engines."*

I slumped back in my chair. "We're sunk, Frank."
"Shhh."

"Robbing a bank is a federal crime," the voice went on.

"Police from coast to coast will be on the lookout for a pair of teenage boys named Frank and Joe."

"Who ride motorcycles," I added.

The TV news reports froze and faded away.

"Of course, American Teens Against Crime realizes that you boys are being framed," the voice continued. *"At this very moment, our agents are investigating the matter, scanning the area for clues and suspects."*

A map filled the screen. Tiny dots lit up across the Northeast coast.

"Until we learn more, we want you boys to lie low," said the voice. *"Find a hiding place and stay there until further notice. Do not, I repeat, do not try to investigate this case on your own."*

I glanced at Frank. His face was locked in a frown.

"This is a very serious matter, boys. Somebody obviously knows who you are. They may even know what you do for the ATAC team. It may be the result of a security leak, and we don't want to take any chances."

Playback the parrot ruffled his feathers. His sudden movement startled me.

"Bad boys!" the bird squawked.

"Playback! Quiet," said Frank, stroking his wing.

How could my brother stay so calm?

We were *WANTED*!

The voice continued, *"Frank and Joe, this is not an assignment. This is a warning. Leave your home immediately. Find a place to hide. And do not contact us with your cell phone. Use the pocket communicator we gave you. We will be sending you daily e-mails to update you on the situation."*

Frank picked up the wireless device and nodded.

"Trust no one," the voice went on. *"Not your friends. Not your family, except for your father, who will understand when you escape. Keep your eyes and ears open at all times."*

I glanced at my brother.

"Above all, remember one thing," said the voice. Our pictures appeared on the screen. *"Frank and Joe Hardy are Wanted."*

A flashing red light flickered behind our photos.

"This disc will be reformatted in five seconds. Four. Three. Two. One."

The screen went blank. A loud rock song blared from the speakers—"Wanted Dead or Alive."

Frank leaned forward and turned off his computer. Then he sat back in his chair and looked at me.

"Start packing," he said. "We have to get out of here. Now."

I stood up. "Where are we going to go?"

Frank shrugged. "How about Dad's old fishing cabin in the mountains? We haven't been there in years."

"Not since Aunt Trudy fell into that patch of poison ivy."

Frank chuckled. "Hurry up. Go pack a bag. We might be gone for a while."

I headed for the door, then stopped. "Frank?"

"Yes?"

"What's going on?" I asked. "Why would someone want to frame us?"

Frank looked at me. "Maybe they're getting revenge. We've put a lot of people behind bars, Joe."

"Yeah. But who?"

Frank held up his hands. "Your guess is as good as mine."

"Maybe it's the bandanna dudes."

My brother laughed. "I don't think those guys are smart enough to rob a bank."

I ran back to my room to grab my backpack. While I was throwing in extra pairs of socks and underwear, I noticed that my cell phone was vibrating.

I had a call.

I was about to push a button on the phone when I remembered something: This could be dangerous.

I shoved my cell into my backpack without answering, zipped it up, and headed back to Frank's room. My brother was almost finished with his packing.

"Do you have room in your backpack for these night goggles?" he asked.

"Sure."

I took the goggles and crammed them inside my pack.

"Ready?"

"Ready."

We opened Frank's door and stepped into the hallway. Quietly we crept to the top of the stairs—and then the doorbell rang.

We froze.

I glanced at Frank. Neither of us moved.

"I'll get it!" Aunt Trudy shouted from the dining room below.

Frank and I peered over the railing and watched Aunt Trudy open the front door.

"Can I help you?"

Two police officers stood in the doorway. "Hello, ma'am," said one of them.

Mom and Dad walked into the foyer.

"What's going on?" asked Mom. "Is there something wrong?"

Dad took a step forward. "John, Bill," he said, extending his hand. "How are you guys doing?"

The officers shook his hand.

"We're fine, Fenton," said the taller cop.

"Did you want to talk to me?" asked Dad.

The officers looked a little nervous. One of them glanced down at the floor while the other spoke.

"Actually, Fenton," he said, "we're looking for your boys, Frank and Joe."

"Frank and Joe?" Dad repeated.

Mom let out a little gasp. "Are they in some sort of trouble?" she asked.

The taller police officer cleared his throat. "We're not sure, ma'am," he said. "We'd like to take them down to the police station for questioning."

4.
Boys on the Run

My brother grabbed my arm.

"What should we do?" he whispered.

I didn't know.

Think, I told myself.

Down at the bottom of the stairs, our parents turned around and glanced up. Joe and I ducked down.

"Frank! Joe!" Mom shouted. "There's someone here to see you!"

Think.

I tried hard to come up with a plan. A second later an idea swooped down out of nowhere—and landed on my shoulder.

Playback.

The parrot ruffled his feathers and rubbed his head against my neck.

"Frank! Joe!"

33

Our parents called up to us. The officers waited patiently by their side.

"We can hear you up there!" said Aunt Trudy.

I reached up and grabbed Playback. Then I tossed the bird down the stairs.

With a loud rustling of wings, the parrot swooped down into the foyer. The police officers let out a startled gasp as the bird circled over their heads.

"Playback!" Aunt Trudy yelled. "Calm down!"

The parrot squawked and flapped at everyone. I could hear their feet shuffling and arms waving in confusion.

"Now's our chance," I said, grabbing Joe's arm. "Let's get out of here."

I led him back to my bedroom and flung open the window.

"What are you doing?" Joe asked.

"Running away."

"Like a wanted criminal?"

"Like a wanted criminal."

I lifted the hinged windowsill, pulled out the hidden rope ladder—always handy in emergencies like this—and unrolled it over the edge. Then, feet first, I climbed out of the window.

"I'm right behind you," said Joe.

We scrambled down to the ground. Squatting low, we raced past the living room window and headed for the driveway.

Joe was about to kick-start his motorcycle when I held up a finger. "Wait," I whispered. "Let's walk our bikes down the street until we're out of earshot."

My brother nodded. Quietly, we pushed our motorcycles down the driveway, past the police car, and onto the road. We were almost at the end of the street when somebody spotted us.

"Hey! Frank! Joe!"

I held my breath and looked over my shoulder.

"Wait up!"

It was our best friend, Chet Morton.

He jogged across his front yard, waving a freckled arm. His face was flushed by the time he reached us.

"What's up, guys?" he asked. "Running from the cops?"

I shot Joe a quick look.

"What do you mean, Chet?" I said.

Our red-haired friend shrugged. "It's all over the news," he explained. "The police are looking for two teenagers named Frank and Joe. In other words, you."

Joe groaned. I glanced around to make sure no one was watching.

"So you robbed a bank, huh?" said Chet, smirking.

"Of course not," I answered.

"Well, next time you should use fake names during the robbery."

"We're innocent, Chet," said Joe.

Chet laughed. "I know. I'm just teasing. I knew you

two would never rob a bank. If you need any help, just let me know."

Joe and I climbed onto our bikes.

"Okay, Chet," I said. "If anyone asks, you didn't see us today. Got it?"

Chet nodded. "Are you going to hide out? I can bring you food and stuff."

"No, thanks," I said. "Really, Chet. You shouldn't get involved."

"Unless you want to be an accomplice to a pair of hardened criminals," Joe added.

Chet smiled. "Good luck, guys. Seriously."

Joe and I revved up our motorcycles and took off. I glanced back at our house before we turned the corner.

The police car was still parked in our driveway.

So far, so good.

Turning back, I leaned forward and gassed it. Joe zoomed along next to me and gave me a thumbs-up.

We're fugitives now.

Shaking the thought from my head, I forced myself to concentrate on the road. Joe and I stayed on the side streets until we were safely out of Bayport. Then we hit the highway at full speed.

Half an hour later Joe started waving at me. Then he pointed at a small mountain in the distance. I couldn't figure out what he was pointing at—until I spotted the police car.

It was about a mile away.

And it was heading right for us.

Joe flashed his turn signal and veered to the right. I followed behind him, slowing down to a stop behind a huge roadside sign for the Bayview Shopping Mall. We turned off our engines and hunched down in the tall grass.

The police car zoomed by.

I let out a long sigh and glanced at Joe. "What are you smiling at?"

My brother shrugged. "I don't know. It's kind of funny. You and me, running from the law."

"I wonder if you'll be laughing in jail."

"Aw, chill out, Frank. They're not going to catch us. We're the undercover brothers, remember?"

"Okay, desperado. Let's roll."

We pushed our motorcycles out of the tall grass, hopped on, and revved them up. Twenty minutes later we reached the mountains. I felt a little safer there, hidden among the tall trees and bushy shrubs. The highway narrowed down to two lanes, winding and curving slowly upward.

We almost missed the turnoff to Dad's cabin.

It was beginning to get dark, and the sign was covered with weeds. I could barely make out the words LAKE MIDNIGHT carved into the wooden post.

Joe and I turned onto the dirt road and headed deeper into the woods. The trees were thicker here, and the path was bumpier. It brought back a lot of memories.

The whole family used to spend our summers at Lake Midnight. Dad was still on the police force, Mom had long hair, and Aunt Trudy used to swim with Joe and me almost every day. We were just kids then, but we knew we wanted to fight crime someday—just like Dad.

Now here we are, I thought.

Our motorcycles rumbled and bounced over the dirt trail. Passing a few small cabins, we were able to see the lake, glistening in the twilight. Minutes later we spotted Dad's fishing cabin.

Joe looked at me and smiled. "Home sweet hide-out."

We pulled our motorcycles around the back to hide them from view. Turning off the engines, we hopped off and removed our helmets.

"The old place looks pretty good," I said, running my fingers through my hair.

"It always looks smaller than I remember it," said Joe.

"That's because for most of the time we spent here, you were just a little pipsqueak."

"With a dorky big brother."

"Who can still beat you up."

"Yeah, right," said Joe. "Bring it on, bro."

I shook my head. "Nah—I think we have enough enemies right now."

We walked around to the front of the cabin. It

wasn't much to look at—just a plain wooden shack with a gray shingle roof. The boards on the front porch creaked as we made our way to the front door.

"Let's see if the key is still here," I said, reaching up to the ledge above the doorway. "Yup."

After unlocking the door, I turned the knob and flung the door open.

BANG!

The wooden slat door slammed against the wall, raising a tiny tornado of dust.

"Whew!" said Joe, coughing. "Aunt Trudy would totally freak out if she saw this."

I waved the dust away and stepped inside. The last rays of dusk beamed through the old curtains, barely illuminating the warped floorboards. I squinted my eyes.

"I wonder if the electricity still works," I said.

Joe flicked a switch next to the door. A dull orange light glowed from a lantern-shaped lamp hanging from the ceiling. "Does that answer your question?"

"Thanks for paying the electric bill, Dad," I muttered.

We threw our backpacks and helmets onto the old leather sofa in front of the stone fireplace. Joe went into the kitchen and turned on another light. He flung open the small refrigerator, then jumped back, holding his nose.

"*Ew*, man! I think Aunt Trudy must have left one of

her world-famous meat loaves in here," he said, gasping for air.

He slammed the door and started snooping through the cupboards. Meanwhile, I reached for the tiny portable TV set next to the sofa. I was surprised to see that it was still working—even though I had to play with the antenna a while before I could see an image.

"We have dried oatmeal," Joe shouted from the kitchen. "And a bag of rice."

"Yum."

Frustrated with the bad reception, I snapped off the TV and flopped back on the sofa. Joe walked out of the kitchen and pointed to the bunk beds in the corner of the living room. This place *was* pretty teeny.

"I claim top bunk," he said.

"The top bunk is mine," I snapped back. "It's always been mine. You know that."

"We're not kids anymore."

I sighed. "Oh, all right. You can have the stupid top bunk."

Joe cheered and scrambled up into the bunk bed. He crossed his legs and kicked back against the pillows. "I like it up here," he said. "How come you never let me sleep on top when we were kids?"

"Because you used to wet the bed."

"Did not."

"Did so."

"Did not."

"Ask Mom. She had to buy plastic sheets for you."

"Liar."

"Bed wetter."

Joe looked like he was about to leap from the bunk to attack me, when his cell phone rang.

"Don't answer it!" I said.

My brother pulled his phone from his pocket and looked at the display screen. "It's Dad."

"Don't answer it," I repeated, climbing into the lower bunk.

"But he's probably worried about us."

"Someone might trace the call."

Joe sighed and let it ring. Finally his voice mail picked up the call. I closed my eyes and started to doze off.

I don't know how long I was asleep, probably about an hour. With my eyes shut, I took in the sounds of wildlife outside.

A bird whistled. Crickets chirped. And . . .

Snap!

. . . something moved in the woods.

I looked at Joe. He heard it too. Then slowly I got up, walked to the door, and turned out the lights.

"What is it, Frank?" my brother whispered in the darkness.

"Shhh."

I waited and listened.

Nothing.

A twig snapped outside. Then another twig.

It sounded like footsteps.

Joe climbed down from the bunk and crept up next to me. Both of us leaned against the door, listening carefully.

The crickets stopped chirping. A bird flapped its wings and flew away.

Then I heard something else.

It sounded like a boy's voice.

I grabbed Joe's arm. "There's somebody out there," I whispered.

5.

Hide and Seek

It's the cops.

That was my first thought.

We're surrounded.

That was my second.

But when I held my breath and listened, I decided that Frank must have been hearing things. "Are you sure you heard—"

"Shhh."

I listened again. This time I heard it.

A boy's voice.

There's somebody out there.

Frank tapped me on the shoulder and waved me toward the sofa. Digging into my backpack, he pulled out a pair of night-vision goggles and crept to the back door of the cabin. It was too dark to see without them.

Good idea.

I grabbed the other pair of goggles from my backpack

and followed Frank. Ducking down, we pushed the back door open and slipped outside. My brother pointed to the left. I headed around that side of the cabin while he went in the other direction.

I slipped the night-vision goggles over my head and peeked around the corner.

Cool.

It was like looking through a kaleidoscope. The woods were bright blue and green with pale yellow splotches.

Then I spotted them.

Two red and orange glowing figures were walking toward the cabin.

Is it them? I wondered. *The bank robbers?*

They stopped and crouched down behind a bush. I glanced around the corner of the cabin and saw Frank. He was glowing orange too—and creeping toward the figures in the bushes.

What was he doing?

It seemed my brother was trying to be some kind of hero by sneaking up on the intruders. Well, if he was planning on tackling them, I figured he would need my help. So I crouched down and crept toward them from the opposite side.

The closer I got, the more I could hear.

"They're inside the cabin," a voice whispered.

"Are you sure? The lights are out," said a second voice.

"They're hiding," said the first voice.

I turned and saw Frank on the other side of the bush. Through the goggles, his whole body glowed bright red.

He looked like he was poised to attack.

I braced myself.

Without warning, Frank let out a loud battle cry.

"AAAAUUGHHH!!!"

He sounded like Geronimo on the warpath.

The two figures jumped back in shock. Frank leaped up and tackled one of them to the ground. I went after the other.

Whump!

We landed with a thud on the soft earth, my opponent kicking and screaming beneath me.

"Hey! Get off me!"

The voice sounded familiar.

I ripped the night-vision goggles off my head, waited for my eyes to adjust, and looked into the face of my enemy.

It was Chet Morton.

"What do you think you're doing?" he asked.

"Yeah, Frank," said a voice next to us. "You're ripping my blouse."

I turned my head—and burst out laughing.

My brother had just tackled Belinda Conrad. She was one of Frank's classmates at school. Beside being blond, bright-eyed, and beautiful, she had a *big* crush on Frank.

"Belinda?" said my brother, gasping, his face nearly pressed against hers. "What are you doing here?"

"I'm getting squashed by a wanted criminal," she responded with a sly smile.

Frank's face turned red.

"Oh! I'm sorry!"

He quickly rolled off Belinda and helped her to her feet.

"What about me?" asked Chet.

"What about you?" I said, still pinning him to the ground. "What are you doing here, Chet? We told you we didn't need your help."

Chet stammered. "I, um . . . we, um . . ."

"We brought food," said Belinda.

"That's a good enough reason for me," I said, crawling off of Chet. "What's for dinner?"

Belinda held up a picnic basket. "I brought my secret-recipe fried chicken and biscuits . . . and all sorts of canned food."

"Did you bring a can opener?" I asked.

"Yes, I did," said Belinda. "Just wait until you try this fried chicken. It's honey-dipped and extra crispy. Do you like fried chicken, Frank?"

Even without the night-vision goggles, I thought I could see my brother blush.

"Yeah, I like fried chicken," he answered. Totally oblivious, as always.

She grinned. "Well, what are you waiting for? Invite

us inside and prepare yourself for a total taste sensation."

Frank chuckled nervously—the way he does whenever he's around a pretty girl—and led us all back to the cabin. My brother, Chet, and I flopped down on the sofa, while Belinda crouched down next to the coffee table.

Boy, was that girl prepared!

She even brought a checkered tablecloth—not to mention canned soda, coleslaw, potato salad, plastic forks and knives, and paper napkins. Best of all were the fried chicken and biscuits.

"Wow," I said, stuffing my face. "This is so good, it's ridiculous! It's crazy! Right, Frank?"

My brother bit into a crispy drumstick, chewed thoughtfully, and nodded. "Totally. Ridiculous. Crazy."

Belinda laughed and dished out second helpings for everyone.

"Thanks a lot," said Frank. "But I'm confused—how did you and Chet find us here?"

Chet started coughing. I slapped him on the back a few times until he was able to speak.

"It's all my fault," he explained. "After you guys left me this afternoon, I hopped in my Mom's car and followed you. It wasn't easy. I had to pull over when you stopped and hid from the police car."

Belinda's eyes widened. "You hid from the police?"

Chet ignored her and continued. "When I saw you

take the road to Lake Midnight, I turned around and came back. I figured you were going to your dad's old fishing cabin. You guys brought me here the summer after fourth grade. Don't you remember?"

"Yeah," I said, thinking back all those years. "Wait, didn't you catch a trout?"

"That's right," said Chet. "Anyway, Belinda was waiting for me when I got back home."

"I know he's a good friend of yours, and I knew you were in big trouble after watching the news about the bank robbery, so I put two and two together," she explained. "I figured he was probably helping you out—or at least knew what the truth was."

"We didn't rob the bank, Belinda," Frank said, frowning.

"Oh, I know," she said. " I figured someone was trying to set you up. Because, you know, you two are the nicest guys in Bayport."

She smiled at Frank, who cleared his throat and blushed yet again.

I started to laugh. "Go on," I said.

"I told Chet that I would go to the cops unless he let me help," Belinda explained.

Chet nodded. "She blackmailed me."

Belinda slapped Chet's arm and turned to Frank. "I only wanted to help. I figured if you and Joe are hiding out from the police, you could use some supplies. Like my secret-recipe fried chicken. So I went home and packed a picnic basket, then Chet drove us here."

We looked at Chet, who lowered his head in shame. "It's all true," he said. "Sorry we scared you."

"Sorry we tackled you," I said.

"Oh, we'll get over it," said Belinda. "And besides, it was kind of fun, wasn't it, Frank?" She nudged my brother.

Frank shifted nervously and wiped his mouth with a napkin. "I didn't mean to rip your blouse, Belinda. I thought you were the bank robbers. There were two of you."

"So I look like a boy?" asked Belinda.

"No," I said. "Frank looks like a girl."

Frank smacked my arm. "No, seriously," he said. "We're in big trouble. Joe and I are being framed by two guys who look exactly like us."

"And the police are looking for two guys who fit our descriptions," I added.

Chet and Belinda glanced at each other.

"They've gotten a little more specific about who they're looking for," said Chet.

"What do you mean?" I asked.

Belinda cleared her throat. "Do you have a television set?"

Frank turned to the side table and snapped on the portable TV set. "The reception is lousy," he said, playing with the antenna. "But we should be able to pick up a local station."

Everyone in the cabin grew silent as Frank played with the knobs. Finally a clear image appeared on the TV screen.

"I can't believe what I'm seeing," I groaned.

There on the screen, in bright yellow letters, was the word WANTED.

Beneath it were two high school photos of Frank and Joe Hardy.

NEWS FLASH

Our top story: Frank and Joe Hardy are wanted for bank robbery.

These are photographs of the two boys who were identified in this morning's bank robbery. Eyewitnesses have confirmed the identities of Frank and Joe Hardy, two local students at Bayport High School. The suspects fled from their Bayport home this afternoon when police tried to bring them in for questioning. They were last seen riding motorcycles and are considered extremely dangerous.

In addition to the robbery of the Bayport Bank, the Hardy brothers are suspected of committing numerous other crimes, including several holdups throughout the area. They also fit the description of two boys who, earlier today, stole dirt bikes and a dune buggy at the Off-Road Vehicle Park on the Jersey Shore.

Police have posted an all-points bulletin. If you have any information about Frank and Joe Hardy, please call . . .

6.

Dirty Rotten Squealers

I turned off the television. Then I sat back, rubbed my eyes, and looked over at Chet and Belinda.

"You two should leave," I said. "Now."

They started to protest. "But . . ."

"Look, guys," I interrupted. "Joe and I are wanted by the police. If you help us out, that makes you accomplices."

Belinda shrugged. "I don't mind, Frank. I'll be your accomplice."

"It's dangerous," I said. "Joe and I are in a lot of trouble. But that doesn't mean you should get into trouble too."

"We're your friends, Frank," said Chet. "We know you're innocent."

"That doesn't matter to the police," I told him. "We've been identified. We're wanted for questioning."

I stood up, walked to the windows, and pulled down the blinds. "Hopefully, nobody followed you here."

"Don't worry," said Chet. "I took a few wrong turns along the way to make sure nobody was behind me."

I nodded and glanced at my watch. "It's getting late. Your parents are going to start wondering where you are."

Chet and Belinda stood up.

"We just want to help, Frank," said Belinda.

"You can help by staying away," I told her in a soft voice. "The police might try to follow you . . . because you're our friends."

Belinda smiled and nodded. I opened the door. Joe and I walked our friends back to the car.

"Oh—don't call our cell phones," I told them. "If we need your help, we'll send you an e-mail."

Chet and Belinda nodded, then waved good-bye. Joe and I watched the car pull away, the headlights flickering and fading into the dark woods.

Joe threw his arm over my shoulder. "Come on. I'll race you back to the hideout."

I was in no mood for a race.

But I couldn't just let him win, could I?

"One, two, three . . . go!"

We took off running toward the cabin, leaping over fallen branches and rocks. The trail was dark, but the finish line was well marked because of the light coming through the cabin doorway. I ran toward it as fast as I could—and almost stumbled when I realized something.

I closed that door when we left the cabin.

Joe dashed ahead of me, stumbling into the doorway and cheering. "I won! I won because you lost!"

"Shhh!"

I came up behind my brother, put a finger to my lips, and waved at him to duck down. Joe looked confused—until he heard the intruder in the cabin.

KA-THUNK!

A steel pot crashed to the floor.

There was someone in the kitchen.

Whoever it was must have been hunched down behind the counter that divided the kitchen from the living room, because I couldn't see anyone from the main room.

But someone was definitely there.

Joe started creeping forward on his hands and knees, sliding up to the counter. I started sneaking around the side.

KA-THUNK!

Another pot crashed onto the floor—and I started to wish I had a weapon of some kind. I looked around, but all I could find was a broom propped against the wall. I grabbed it and took another step.

Joe looked at me and held up three fingers. Then he started counting down.

Three, two . . .

I guess he planned to jump the guy in the kitchen. I wasn't sure it was such a good idea, but what choice did I have?

One!

Joe leaped up onto the counter and shouted, "Freeze!"

I jumped into the kitchen, holding the broom like a baseball bat, and faced the intruder.

Yikes.

It was a raccoon.

Not a cute little baby raccoon, no. This was a giant, full-grown, sharp-toothed, pointy-clawed adult that must have been at least three feet long!

The raccoon hissed.

And attacked.

Me.

"Look out, Frank!"

Thanks, Joe.

I really didn't need to be told to "look out"—not when a monster rodent was charging right at me, baring its fangs.

WHOOSH!

I swung the broom through the air and . . .

WHAP!

I swatted that huge raccoon's big furry butt toward the door.

"Way to go, Frank!"

The raccoon let out a loud yelp and took off running

toward the open doorway. As soon as its bushy black tail crossed the threshold, Joe jumped off the kitchen countertop and slammed the door.

My heart was pounding. "Lock the door, Joe," I said. "Please."

"Man! Could you believe the size of that thing?"

I flopped down on the sofa, trying to catch my breath.

"Those fangs! That hissing! Man!"

I closed my eyes and rubbed my forehead.

"Was it scary, Frank? Seeing those big teeth and claws coming at you?"

I opened my eyes. "What do you think, Joe?"

"I think you were so scared, you almost wet yourself."

"*You're* the bed wetter, Joe."

My brother responded by jumping on top of me, hissing and baring his teeth.

"Knock it off!" I yelled, pushing him away. "Go clean up the mess in the kitchen. That raccoon scattered chicken bones all over the floor."

"Well, you can't blame him," said Joe, standing up. "Your girlfriend makes mighty fine fried chicken."

"Belinda's not my girlfriend."

"Okay, sorry. She's your *accomplice*."

I ignored him and reached for my backpack. I figured I should check our e-mail to see if we'd received any messages from ATAC. So I pulled out the pocket communicator and flipped it on.

"Hey, Joe. We got a message," I yelled toward the kitchen.

"From ATAC?" he shouted back.

"I think so."

My brother came in from the kitchen, wiping his hands with a dish towel and flopping into an armchair. "What's it say?"

I read the message out loud:

To: TheWanted1s
From: AmTeenHQ
Re: Congratulations

Good job, boys. You've managed to evade the police. We assume you've found a good hiding place. Just lie low and we will take care of things. We are investigating several suspects, including the criminals you have apprehended in your past missions. So far all of them are accounted for. Let us know if you have any clues to the robbers' identities. In the meantime, stay hidden, don't go out in public, and do NOT try to solve this case on your own. Remember: TRUST NO ONE.

I finished reading and looked up at Joe.

"Trust no one?" he said. "Not even pretty girls who bring us fried chicken?"

I shook my head. "Belinda and Chet are security risks, Joe. They know where we're hiding."

My brother waved me off. "They would never tell."

"It's not that. I just don't like the idea of them getting involved."

"You just don't like getting involved with *Belinda*."

"Give me a break, Joe."

"She likes you, Frank! She's dying to go out on a date with you! Why don't you ask her?"

"Yeah, right. I can just hear myself." I held an imaginary phone to my ear. "Hello, Belinda? This is Frank Hardy, wanted criminal. How'd you like to flee from justice on Saturday night?"

Joe laughed. "You know she'd say yes. Girls really dig the 'bad boy' types."

"Yeah, that's me. Frank 'Bad Boy' Hardy."

"Bad *breath*, maybe."

"Very funny," I said, glancing down at the pocket communicator. "We have another message."

"Really? From who?"

"From DaddyO."

"Oh. Read it."

I read the message aloud:

To: TheWanted1s
From: DaddyO
Re: Relax

Hi, boys. Hope you're okay. The ATAC team called me as soon as the police left, and they explained your situation. I don't know who would try to frame you, but I have a few ideas. I'll fill you in later. Mom and Aunt Trudy are a little upset, of course, but they don't believe you're guilty. Everyone's worried about you. Myself included. Just stay in contact with ATAC, and DON'T GO SNOOPING AROUND.

I looked at Joe and smirked. "Dad knows us too well," I said.

"Yeah," said Joe. "We can't just sit back and let those creeps drag our names through the mud. We have to do something."

"But if we try to investigate, we'll be recognized. The police put out an all-points bulletin on two teenage boys with motorcycles."

"We could split up."

"We could also follow instructions and stay here."

Joe was about to argue with me when we were interrupted by an electronic *bling* sound.

There was another e-mail message on the communicator.

"You've got mail," said Joe, in a deep, robotic voice.

"No kidding."

"Who's it from? ATAC? DaddyO? Chet?"

I looked down at the e-mail's return address. "You're not going to believe this."

"What? Aunt Trudy hacked into our system?"

"No," I told him. "The robbers did."

"What?"

I read him the message:

To: The Wanted1s
From: FranknJoe
Re: America's Most Wanted Teens
Hello there, wanted ones. So now the whole world thinks
that Frank and Joe Hardy are criminals. Hardy-har-har!
Now you know what it's like, you dirty rotten squealers!
Revenge is sweet. But just wait. It's going to get sweeter.
Signed, "Frank" and "Joe."

"How did they get this e-mail address?" Joe asked.

"I don't know. It's brand-new."

"I don't like the looks of this, Frank."

"Me neither," I said, studying the message again.
"And I especially don't like the looks of *this*."

"What?"

"They wrote a P.S."

"Yeah? What is it?"

I read the final sentence.

"P.S. We know where you're hiding."

7.
Send in the Clowns

I couldn't sleep that night.

Every little sound outside the cabin—every hooting owl, every fluttering moth—made me jump up in bed.

Is it them? Are they here?

Then I'd look around the dark cabin and feel a little stupid for getting all worked up.

If they know where we're hiding, then why don't they come and get us?

I tried to go back to sleep. But as soon as I started to doze off, Frank's snoring woke me up again.

"Dude! Stop snoring!" I yelled down to the lower bunk.

Frank mumbled something about "chicken" and rolled over, still snoring.

Then I tried counting sheep. Which didn't work at all because the sheep kept turning into Wanted posters with my face on them.

Before I knew it, I was being shaken awake.

"Rise and shine, Joe. We've got work to do."

I rubbed my eyes. Sunlight was streaming through the window, and Frank was standing at the counter, typing into the pocket communicator.

"Are you going to sleep all day?" he asked. "Get up!"

"I was up all night," I groaned, throwing my feet over the side of the bunk. "Your snoring kept me awake."

"I never snore."

"And I never wet the bed."

I crawled down from the bunk and approached the counter. "Who are you e-mailing?"

"Chet and Belinda."

"Really? I thought you didn't want them to get involved."

"Well, we need their help now."

Frank clicked send, then brought up another e-mail on the screen.

"This one was sent to us this morning," he said, handing the communicator to me.

I looked down and read the message.

To: TheWanted1s
From: FranknJoe
Re: Hardy Heist!!!
Have you heard the news, boys? The Hardy brothers are plotting a jewel heist! Where? Bayport Jewelers! When? Two o'clock this afternoon! Why? Because those boys are

SO BAD! SOMEBODY SHOULD STOP THEM!

Signed, "Frank" and "Joe"

P.S. Don't call the cops OR YOU'LL BE SORRY!

"It's a trap, Frank," I said.

"I know."

"So what are we going to do?"

"We're going to walk right into it."

"You're kidding."

"I never kid about walking into traps."

"But Frank, I thought you wanted us to follow instructions and stay here in the hideout."

"I changed my mind."

"All right!"

Game on.

I was glad Frank had changed his mind. I couldn't stand just waiting around in this cabin, not doing anything, while those two creeps were committing robberies and using our names.

It's payback time.

I glanced down at the pocket communicator and noticed that Frank had written a couple of other e-mails.

"You already told Dad and the ATAC team what you're planning to do?"

"No, not yet," Frank explained. "I wrote those to be sent later automatically. They won't receive the e-mails until two o'clock this afternoon."

"When our evil twins are robbing the jewelry store."

Frank laughed. "I like that. Evil twins. Ha!" He grabbed a towel from the closet, dusted it off a little, and headed for the bathroom. "I'm going to take a quick shower. Keep a lookout."

I walked to the kitchen and looked inside Belinda's picnic basket. Frank had already opened—and finished off—a can of sliced pineapples. Which left me with . . .

Oh, great.

. . . baked beans, creamed corn, or beets.

I dug deeper into the basket until I found a leftover biscuit from last night. It was a little hard, but anything was better than canned beets. I opened my mouth, took a bite—and almost choked.

Not because of the biscuit.

Because somebody was staring at me through the kitchen window.

"It's the police! Come out with your hands up!"

It wasn't the police.

It was Chet, waving and smiling.

Right behind him was Belinda, carrying two large shopping bags.

"Let us in, Joe!" said Chet.

"No!" I shouted through the window. "You almost gave me a heart attack!"

"We brought donuts," said Belinda.

I threw the door open. "What kind? Jelly? Cream?"

"Assorted," said Belinda, waltzing into the cabin and setting down her packages. "Where's Frank?"

"In the shower."

The three of us gobbled donuts and drank orange juice while Frank finished his shower. A few minutes later he emerged, wearing nothing but a towel and a sheepish look on his face.

"Do you mind turning around while I put on my clothes, Belinda?" asked Frank.

"Not at all," she replied. "I'll show Joe the costumes I brought for you."

"Costumes?" I asked.

"Yeah," said Frank, slipping into his shorts. "I don't want anybody to recognize us today. Not even our evil twins. I mean, we could just show up and confuse the cops, since there'll be four Hardys. But I have another idea."

"Okay," I said. "What kind of costumes?"

Belinda reached into her shopping bags and pulled out two bright red wigs. "Ta-da!"

"What are those?"

"Clown wigs," she said. "And look. Clown shoes, too."

Frank and I were in shock.

Belinda just giggled as she pulled the rest of the clown outfits out of the bags. "My mom and dad wore these to a costume party last year."

Frank walked over and picked up a wig. "We want to be disguised, Belinda. Not stick out like sore thumbs."

She sat back and crossed her arms. "Do you think

I'm stupid? These are the *perfect* disguises . . . because today is the Bayport Summer Day Parade!"

I looked at Frank. He scratched his chin.

"There'll be clowns *everywhere*," Belinda added.

Frank shrugged. "Actually, that's a great idea."

I couldn't believe my brother was going along with this. "You're kidding. Right, Frank?"

He looked at me. "Our doubles won't expect us to dress up as clowns. That's for sure."

"And once I put some greasepaint on your faces," said Belinda, "*nobody* will recognize you. Not even your own parents."

I slumped down into the sofa. "Okay," I groaned. "I'm game if you are, Frank."

Belinda grinned. Then she pulled a small makeup kit out of a shopping bag and rubbed her hands together. "Okay, you clowns. Let's get to work."

Forty-five minutes later, Frank and I looked like a pair of total Bozos.

"I feel ridiculous," I said. "And this stupid rubber nose is pinching me."

"Shut up or I'll turn you into one of those sad clowns," said Belinda, applying the final touches of lipstick to my mouth.

Frank hopped around, testing out his big, floppy clown shoes. "How do I look?"

"Scary," said Chet.

We turned and looked at him.

Chet shrugged. "I've always been afraid of clowns."

Frank bent over and pulled three small balls out of Belinda's shopping bag. "Cool. We can juggle." He tossed the balls into the air but only managed to catch four tosses before the balls bounced on the floor.

"Here. Let me show you how it's done." I picked up the balls and started juggling like a pro.

Frank reached into the bag and pulled out a giant squeeze horn. He honked it right in my face, and I dropped the balls.

Belinda laughed and clapped her hands. "You guys are naturals."

Chet covered his face. "As I said. Scary!"

We reached Bayport by one thirty. The parade was already in full swing—which made it impossible for Chet to find a parking space. The whole town square was mobbed with cheering spectators and marching bands and fire trucks and floats.

"Just let us off here," said Frank. "We don't want to miss the jewel heist."

Belinda turned around and said, "Good luck." She was sitting in the front seat with Chet because our red wigs and floppy shoes filled up the entire back seat. "Break a leg," she added. "Make 'em laugh!"

Frank and I crawled out of the car and stepped onto the sidewalk.

"Look, Mommy! Clowns!" shouted a little girl.

"Okay, Joe. We're on," Frank whispered.

I made a goofy face and started juggling. My brother pulled out the squeeze horn and honked away.

The little girl burst into tears.

"I hate clowns! Mommy!"

Frank turned and looked at me. "Some children have no sense of humor. Come on. Let's head for the jewelry store. It's on the other side of the square."

I glanced at my watch. "We still have fifteen minutes."

"According to mine, we have only ten," he said. "We should synchronize our watches."

I started laughing. "Sorry, Frank. It's hard to take you seriously with that clown face."

Frank grumbled. "It's hard to take *you* seriously . . . period."

We set our watches to match the giant clock on the courthouse building and started working our way through the crowd.

I'll tell you, it wasn't easy. Children kept grabbing us, and parents kept asking us to pose for photos. One little brat even tried to pull off my red rubber nose.

The things you have to do for justice.

"There it is!" said Frank, nudging me. "Bayport Jewelers."

The jewelry store was small and quaint—and across the street. That was a problem, because the street was packed with baton twirlers.

"We can't cross the street," I said, leaning against a police barricade. "We'll be clubbed to death by batons."

"But it's almost two o'clock. We have to risk it."

"If you say so, Bozo."

Without hesitating, I leaned on the barricade and kicked up my feet. The big, floppy shoes swung over the top, landing on the street with a loud clap. Frank was right behind me.

"Here goes nothing," I said.

We plunged into the mob of strutting baton twirlers. "Sorry . . . excuse me . . . sorry . . . excuse me."

Batons whirled and twirled past our heads. One of them hit me on the head, but it didn't hurt because of the fluffy red wig. Frank started honking his horn, blazing a trail through the marching majorettes. "This way, Joe!" he yelled.

I stumbled after him, and seconds later we reached the other side of the street.

"Here we are," said Frank. "Bayport Jewelers."

"And it's two o'clock," I pointed out.

"Come on. Let's check it out." Frank walked to the entrance of the small jewelry store, pushed open the door, and stopped in his tracks.

Someone screamed.

"Help! I'm being robbed!"

And then the store's alarm went off.

POLICE BULLETIN

June 15, 2:05 p.m.
ROBBERY IN PROGRESS

ATTENTION: all parade security officers.
The police alarm has been triggered at
Bayport Jewelers in the town square.

All available officers: Surround the
building and secure the area. There may
be a robbery in progress, so approach the
crime scene with extreme caution.

Repeat: Approach with extreme caution.

Over and out.

8.

Runaway Parade

The alarm was so loud I could barely hear what Joe shouted in my ear.

I think he said, "Frank! There they are!"

He pointed at the jewel counter across the room. An older bald gentleman stood with his hands in the air, trembling and shaking his head.

In front of him stood two teenage boys.

Our evil twins.

They were the same height and build as Joe and myself, one blond, the other dark-haired. And yes, they looked a *lot* like us.

The evil "Joe" was holding open a burlap sack while the evil "Frank" scooped in jewelry from the glass case. They looked up and saw us.

"What are you clowns looking at?" barked the older teenager.

I had almost forgotten about our disguises.

But hey, they seemed to work. Our diabolical doubles didn't seem to realize who we were.

Until Joe shouted at them. "Imposters! Stop impersonating us!"

"Joe" and "Frank" stopped loading the sack with jewels.

"It's them," growled the younger boy. Closing his sack and digging in his heels, he charged at my brother.

The other one came after me.

"Out of our way, clowns!" yelled my look-alike.

WHAM!

The pair of robbers slammed into us like a wall of defensive linemen in a football game.

CRASH!

Joe and I staggering backward, knocking over two glass cases filled with diamond necklaces. The jewelry spilled across the floor at our feet.

"We'll take those," said the older boy, snatching up a handful of necklaces.

Then he and his blond-haired partner turned and ran from the store.

I tried to get up as fast as I could—which was hard to do in a baggy clown suit and floppy shoes. Joe was pinned beneath the fallen display case, his fuzzy red wig flattened against the glass. Lifting the corner, I was able to free him.

"Quick! They're getting away!" Joe shouted.

We turned toward the front door and stopped.

"Freeze! You're under arrest!"

Two police officers blocked the doorway.

Joe slapped my arm and dashed to the back of the store. I had no idea what he was doing but followed along anyway. First he pushed past the baldheaded storeowner and ran into the stockroom. Then he kicked open the rear fire exit and dashed out into a back alley.

"Good job," I said, rushing after him.

We slammed the fire door shut and pushed a couple of garbage cans in front of it. We could hear the two cops pounding on the other side of the door.

"Stop in the name of the law!"

Spinning around, we searched for an escape route.

Easier said than done.

Another pair of police officers ran straight toward us down the alley. Joe and I turned and ran the other way, our floppy clown shoes slapping hard on the concrete street. I could hear the two officers right behind us—so I knocked a few trash cans into their path.

"Oof! Augh!"

The cops stumbled and fell—*splat*—into a heaping pile of steaming garbage.

"Way to go," Joe yelled, glancing back.

Running after him, I looked down toward the other end of the alley—and winced.

We were heading right into the middle of the parade.

Now, I hate parades. But hey, it's better to be in a parade than in jail, right?

Charging full steam ahead, Joe and I bounded out of the alley—and straight into a marching band. The band members were wearing Bayport High School Band uniforms and playing "Seventy-Six Trombones." They were well trained, marching in perfect unison. But they weren't prepared for two clowns like Joe and me.

"Whoa! Look out!"

Joe collided belly-first with a tuba player. I got poked in the red rubber nose by a flutist. Bouncing off her, I spun around and slammed into a tiny clarinetist— who was not amused.

"Sorry," I said, trying to get in line—and in step— with the rest of the band.

Joe was trying to do the same thing, but a nerdy-looking trumpeter kept knocking him out of the way.

I glanced at the crowds of people on either side of the parade route. Everyone was cheering and clapping— except for a bunch of cops who were heading right for us.

"Joe! Run!" I yelled.

Using our oversize wigs like battering rams, we plowed our way through the marching band until we reached the last column of marchers. Then we found ourselves face-to-face with a fire truck.

"Look out, Frank!" Joe yelled.

The fire truck blared its horn. I jumped out of the way in the nick of time. Joe grabbed my arm, and we started to run along the length of the fire truck. But we smashed into a human blockade of four burly police officers.

We had nowhere to go—but up.

I grabbed my squeeze horn and honked it in the officer's faces. Then I spun around and started to climb up the side of the fire truck. Joe was already ahead of me. He reached down and gave me a hand, hauling me up on top of the moving truck.

The crowd cheered.

And, since we were dressed like clowns, we acted like clowns. I honked my horn at the kids and Joe juggled his balls while we carefully made our way to the back of the truck. A couple of cops started climbing up the sides.

"Hurry!" Joe yelled. "This way! Jump!"

I didn't know what my brother was talking about—until I watched him run the full length of the engine's ladder and dive through air.

A cop grabbed my ankle, but I shook it off. And I didn't waste any time getting off that fire truck, either. In those big floppy shoes, I made a mad dash across the ladder, diving off the end and . . .

SPLAT!

I landed next to Joe on a huge flower-covered float. Petals flew everywhere.

"Glad you could join me," said Joe.

I was about to answer him when a giant archway of roses collapsed on top of us.

WHUMP!

There were flowers everywhere—in the air, in my mouth, in our wigs. But that was the least of our problems.

A police officer was climbing up onto the float.

"Freeze!"

Yeah, right.

Two undercover agents wearing wigs and greasepaint on a hot summer day are *not* going to freeze.

Instead, we lifted the rose-petal arch up, up, and over until—*BAM*—it clobbered the officer in the head and knocked him down.

Joe and I tried to stand up on the moving float—it wasn't easy. But *running* on a moving float is pretty easy when you see a bunch of cops coming after you.

We scrambled to the back of the float—and leaped.

WHAM! WHAM!

Both of us belly flopped onto the front hood of a big, shiny convertible. It was one of those cars they use in parades to drive around celebrities who wave at the crowd. And sure enough, this one featured the Bayport homecoming queen and prom queen.

The two girls started screaming when Joe and I scrambled over the windshield and into the car.

"What do you think you're doing?"

"Hey! Get out of our car!"

They started beating us with bouquets of flowers. I honked back at them with my horn. The driver, who sat next to us in the front seat, seemed to be in a state of shock. Joe grabbed the wheel from him.

"Sorry, but we're in a hurry, man," he told the driver. "Step on it."

Joe slammed his big, floppy shoe down on the accelerator, shoving the other guy's foot out of the way. The car jerked and jumped forward, spinning off the street and onto the curb.

"Look out!"

The crowd screamed and leaped out of the way. The homecoming queen and prom queen ducked down in the backseat, and the car surged forward.

CRUNCH!

The front fender of the convertible crashed through the police barricade. The whole car bounced up onto the sidewalk and careened toward the middle of the town square.

"Joe! Look out!" I yelled.

It was too late. We were barreling straight for the huge fountain in the square.

SPLASH!

The whole car lurched forward—and plunged into the fountain. Water sprayed through the air, dousing us in a geyser and flooding the wrecked vehicle.

"My hair! It's ruined!" wailed one of the queens.

"Your hair? What about my dress?" shouted the other queen.

The girls turned and glared at Joe and me.

"Who *are* you clowns?" asked the prom queen.

We weren't about to stick around to answer her question—not when a whole squadron of cops was racing toward the fountain.

"Let's get out of here," I said.

Joe and I hopped out of the car and waded through the fountain. A crowd of people had gathered around, and we had to push our way through to get out.

"Stop them! Stop those clowns!"

The police started sprinting after us. Joe and I stumbled through the crowd, looking for a way to escape. A baby screamed as I ran by, and its mother yelled after us, "You should be ashamed of yourselves!"

Don't worry, lady, I thought. *This is the most shameful day of my life.*

I thought we were done for. The police were closing in on us. The parade had come to a halt. People were pushing and shoving, left and right. There was nowhere left to hide.

And then a miracle happened.

A troupe of clowns appeared in front of us.

"Joe!" I shouted. "Head for the clowns!"

Holding on to our wigs, we dove into the middle of the troupe. The clowns scattered as the police swarmed around us.

"There he is!"

"No, that's not him!"

"Him?"

"No! The suspect has a red nose, not a blue one!"

"But almost all of them have red noses!"

It was total chaos—and a perfect opportunity for Joe and me to slip away. Sneaking past a confused cop, we tiptoed onto the sidewalk and ducked into an alley.

"Hurry!" Joe shouted. "We can outrun them!"

"In these shoes?"

"Sure! Come on!"

I followed him down the alley and started running. We glanced over our shoulders to make sure we weren't being followed.

No such luck.

"There they are! They're getting away!" an officer shouted behind me. He started chasing after us.

"Relax," said another cop. "They're not getting away."

I didn't understand his comment—until I turned my head and looked down the alley.

It was a dead end.

9.

Against the Wall

"Stop right there!" a police officer shouted.

Dude, I thought. *We have no choice. We're backed against the wall.*

"Now turn around slowly with your hands in the air!"

This isn't happening.

I looked up at the tall brick wall in front of me, then glanced over at Frank.

"Okay, Mr. Know-It-All. What do we do now?"

My brother took a deep breath. "I don't know, Joe. Do you have any ideas?"

"We could plead insanity."

"It would explain the clown outfits."

We could hear the officers' footsteps coming up behind us. "Hands in the air, boys!"

Slowly we began to raise our hands.

"Don't make any sudden moves," said a deep-voiced officer.

This is not cool.

I wasn't looking forward to being fingerprinted, photographed, and thrown into a jail cell. The last thing I wanted was to have my mug shot taken while wearing clown makeup.

How embarrassing.

"You have the right to remain silent."

The cops were about fifteen feet behind us.

"This is it, Frank," I whispered to my brother. "We're going to jail."

"No, we're not," he said, nodding upward. "Look."

A long rope ladder dangled down from the brick wall.

"We're out of here!" Frank said, grabbing the ladder and scrambling up.

I was right behind him, poking my floppy shoes through the rope rungs and pulling myself up as fast I could.

"Hey! Wait!" shouted one of the cops.

"They're getting away!"

The police started running toward us, lunging at the swinging ladder.

But Frank and I were too quick for them.

Ha!

Frank disappeared over the wall, landing with a loud *thump* on the other side. I swung my leg over the top, then pulled the rope ladder up behind me. The police officers jumped and tried to grab it—but missed.

"You'll never take us alive, coppers!" I yelled as I leaped from the wall.

I landed hard on the other side, tumbling in a heap at Frank's feet.

"You'll never take us alive, coppers'?" said Frank, looking down at me. "What are you, a gangster?"

I shrugged. "I've always wanted to say that."

My brother gave me a hand to help me up. Then we turned around to see who had rescued us with the rope ladder.

"Dad?"

Our father stood in front of us, rolling up the rope ladder and shaking his head.

I couldn't have been more surprised.

Dad? Aiding and abetting wanted criminals?

"Follow me," he said, wasting no time. Waving us forward, he led us past the back of a restaurant, around the corner, and into the street.

His car was parked next to the curb—with the engine still running.

"Hop in, you clowns."

Frank and I dove into the backseat. Dad jumped behind the wheel and hit the gas, the tires screeching on the pavement as we tore off down the road. After a few sharp turns, we were leaving Bayport and zooming down the highway.

"Thanks, Dad," I said.

"Thank yourselves," he replied. "It's your rope ladder.

I had to hide it from the police after you made your escape yesterday."

He flashed the turn signal and steered onto an exit ramp.

"Where are we going?" I asked.

"Back to your hideout," my father answered. "You're staying at my old fishing cabin, right?"

"Yeah," I said. "How did you know?"

"I used to be a police detective, remember?"

"How could we forget?" I said, winking at my brother.

"Nice disguises, by the way."

Frank and I started laughing. "This greasepaint is really gross," I said. "Isn't there a pack of tissues in the glove compartment?"

Dad opened the compartment and tossed the pack back to us. "Here you go."

Frank and I tore off our wigs and started wiping the clown makeup from our faces.

"I got your e-mail, Frank," Dad said, glancing at us in the rearview mirror. "I should have known you guys wouldn't listen to the ATAC team's instructions."

My brother sighed. "You're not mad at us, are you?"

Dad shook his head. "I knew you wouldn't be able to just hide out and do nothing. You're Hardys. You solve crimes. It's in your blood."

"We're just following in our father's footsteps," I said.

"Hey, don't try to pin this on *me*. I'm not wanted for robbery."

"No, but you're an accomplice now," Frank pointed out.

"True."

Frank and I finished removing as much of the makeup as we could. It felt good to get that stuff off my face. My poor nose was aching from wearing the red rubber one.

"Did you boys get to see the suspects today?" Dad asked.

"Yes," said Frank. "We caught them in the act while they were robbing the jewelry store."

"Describe them."

"They looked just like Joe and me. Same ages. Same heights. Same builds."

"Yeah, but my look-alike wasn't a real blond," I added. "His hair was ratty from a bad dye job. It wasn't streaky and natural like mine."

"Oh, get over yourself," said Frank, rolling his eyes.

"*You* get over yourself."

Our father interrupted. "He's got a point, Frank. The dyed hair is a clue. Good observation, Joe."

I smirked at Frank.

"So tell me," Dad continued. "What happened when you walked in on them robbing the store?"

Frank and I glanced at each other and sighed.

"They knocked us down and ran away," I admitted.

"Joe got pinned beneath a display case," Frank said, laughing.

"It's not funny. My elbow is bruised."

Dad chuckled. "Well, you can recover at the cabin. Those big bad bullies won't find you there."

I glanced at Frank. "Maybe we should tell Dad about the e-mail."

"What e-mail?" asked Dad.

"The suspects somehow got our new e-mail address," I explained. Then I told him all about the message we'd received last night from "Frank" and "Joe." "They called us 'dirty rotten squealers' and said, 'We know where you're hiding.'"

Dad's face turned pale. "Dirty rotten squealers?"

"Yeah."

My father didn't say anything. But I could tell he was upset.

"What's wrong, Dad?"

He cleared his throat. "I think I know who the imposters are."

Frank and I bolted up in our seats. "Who?"

Dad took a deep breath. "It's a long story," he began. "And it started a long time ago. Before you boys were born."

I gave Frank a puzzled look.

What was this all about? Was Dad in some sort of trouble?

He continued. "I joined the police force right after I

married your mother. Man, I loved my job. And I loved my partner, too. His name was Jake Johansen, and he was a former football star from Boston. From the moment we met, we were best buddies. We used to do everything together—go fishing, play ball, take our families on picnics. Our wives became good friends too. They both got pregnant at the same time. Yeah, those were the days. Our families were like a pair of matching bookends. We each had two baby boys and promising careers on the force."

Dad paused.

"That's when everything started to go wrong."

He stared at the road and said nothing more. I glanced nervously at my brother.

"What happened, Dad?" I asked.

He sighed. "Things started disappearing from the crime scenes we investigated. Money, jewelry, watches. At first I thought the people involved were lying about the thefts. Most of them were criminals, after all. But then, one day, I caught a glimpse inside Jake's locker. It was filled with all the stolen articles. I guess he liked trying to get away with sneaking behind our backs. But the game was over when I figured out that my partner—my best friend—was a common thief."

"What did you do?" I asked.

Dad frowned. "I didn't want to turn Jake in. So I tried to talk to him about it, give him the benefit of the doubt. At first he denied everything. Finally, he admitted that he might have a problem—some sort of crazy compulsion to steal. He promised me he would get some professional counseling. He also promised he would never steal again."

"Let me guess," I said. "He lied."

My father nodded. "If anything, he got worse. He even began stealing evidence from the police department. It turned out that suspects were paying him off. He was sabotaging cases and getting rich doing it. After a few months, I couldn't take it anymore."

"You turned him in?" I asked.

My father nodded slowly. "I even testified against him during the internal affairs investigation."

I looked at Frank. "That must have been tough, Dad. Testifying against your best friend."

Dad sighed. "The guy was pretty messed up. It was really awful to see him fall. At his trial, he went nuts, screaming and yelling at me, calling me a 'dirty rotten squealer.' As they dragged him out of the courtroom, he looked at me and said, 'I'm going to get you, Hardy. You and your little family, too.'"

I shook my head. "Wow."

"Yeah, wow," said Dad. "I never told you guys about it because, I don't know, you were just babies. Jake was sent to prison upstate, and his wife and kids—two baby boys, like you—moved away. There was never any reason to bring it up."

We sat there in silence for a while. Dad turned onto

the road to Lake Midnight and started driving up the bumpy trail toward the cabin.

"So Jake is out of jail now?" I asked.

"He was let out years ago," Dad answered. "I heard that he moved to California."

"And you think he enlisted his kids to get revenge on our family?"

Dad nodded grimly.

"I just thought of something," Frank said, leaning forward. "You and Jake used to go fishing together. So he knows about the cabin?"

"Yeah. We used to fish here every weekend."

"So maybe it's not the best hideout," said Frank. "Since it's perfect."

"No, it's not," said Dad. "Unless you want to catch these guys."

"So you're suggesting . . ."

"I'm suggesting that we set a trap for them before they get here."

All right, Dad!

I *knew* he'd want us to catch these creeps ourselves.

Pulling up next to the cabin, Dad parked the car and opened the door. Frank and I jumped out and tore off the clown clothes in about five seconds flat. It was a relief to feel the air on my legs.

"Where are your motorcycles?" Dad asked, walking toward the cabin door.

"We hid them around back," I told him. "So tell us,

Dad. How should we prepare for these guys? Set some booby traps? Surprise them with an ambush?"

My father threw open the cabin door, took a step inside, then suddenly stopped.

"Well, boys. You can forget about surprising them," he said.

"Why? What do you mean?"

Frank and I took a look inside the cabin.

"No way," my brother groaned.

The place had been totally ransacked.

Every piece of furniture in the cabin was overturned. Our backpacks had been emptied out, everything scattered across the floor. Even the kitchen drawers had been pulled out and dumped.

But that wasn't the worst of it.

The vandals had spray-painted all over the walls. In huge, splotchy letters were the words *guilty*, *wanted*, and *dirty rotten squealers*.

But creepiest of all was the message above the fireplace:

YOU'RE DEAD.

ROBBERS ON THE RAMPAGE!
Clown Caper Causes Parade Pandemonium

(*Bayport County News*) Bayport's annual Summer Day Parade became the scene of crime and chaos this afternoon when a gang of teenage robbers held up Bayport Jewelers in the town square. "We thought there were only two of them," reported Officer Jones of the Bayport Police. "But now we have reason to believe that they're working with two other unidentified boys. Dressed as clowns, the pair created a distraction while the jewel thieves made their escape." The two clowns destroyed the Bayport Florist float and then carjacked a convertible carrying Bayport High School's homecoming queen and prom queen. Crashing the car into the town square fountain, the suspects ruined the girls' dresses and brought the annual parade to a tragic end. If you have any information regarding the wanted criminals, Frank and Joe Hardy—as well as their clown-faced accomplices—please contact the Bayport Police.

10.
Ambushed!

YOU'RE DEAD.

The words sent a chill up my spine. Just the idea that they had broken into our cabin and trashed the place made me want to scream. But all I could do was stand there and stare at the spray-painted threats on the walls.

"I wonder if they stole our stuff," said Joe. "Like the pocket communicator and night goggles."

"I don't know. Let's see."

I walked into the room and started picking things up off the floor. Our spare clothes were scattered everywhere. Dad and Joe set the toppled chairs and tables upright, tossing a blanket over the sofa.

It had been slashed with a knife.

"I found our backpacks," I said, reaching behind the armchair. I picked them up and looked inside. "Guess what? They didn't take our goggles or binoculars."

Dad didn't seem surprised. "They didn't come here to burglarize the place, boys," he said. "They did it to scare you."

Joe picked up a lamp and looked at me. "How about the pocket communicator?"

I peeked inside the backpacks. "It's not in here."

We went back to straightening the place. It took about an hour to get it looking halfway decent—even though the graffiti on the walls remained as a grim reminder of our situation: We were wanted by the police and targeted by a trio of dangerous thugs.

I'd given up hope of finding the communicator when I suddenly noticed a flashing green light beneath the sofa. "Look what I found," I said, reaching under and pulling out the communicator.

"I'm surprised they left it here," said Joe.

"I'm not," I said. "They left us a message."

I handed the communicator to Joe. The small screen was blinking on and off, flashing a message in large blocky letters:

THIS IS JUST A WARNING. WE'RE WATCHING YOU.

Joe erased the message with the click of a button. "Thugs," he muttered. "Hey, look. We got an e-mail from ATAC."

"Read it," I said.

Joe double-clicked and read the message aloud:

To: TheWanted1s

From: AmTeenHQ

Re: The 411

Hey, guys. Sorry about what happened at the parade today. If you had sent your e-mail sooner, we could have posted some of our agents at the crime scene. We're a little disappointed that you ignored our instructions. But we'll discuss that later.

We have identified the culprits who are "borrowing" your identities. Their names are Fred and Jim Johansen, and they are the sons of your father's former partner on the police force, Jake Johansen.

Jake was released from prison ten years ago. He reunited with his wife and sons, then relocated to San Diego, California. Last year, a string of robberies in the San Diego area was traced to the Johansen family. The mother was innocent of the crimes, however, and agreed to cooperate with the police. But Jake and his sons managed to slip away before the police could apprehend them.

With this e-mail, we've attached documents that include photographs and news stories about the Johansen family. Please look them over—and be on the lookout.

They have a score to settle with you and your family.

Joe finished reading. I glanced up at Dad. His whole face was tensed up, his eyes fixed on the screen.

My brother double-clicked on the documents that

were attached to the e-mail. A bunch of windows started popping open, filling the small screen with newspaper headlines and black-and-white photos.

The first article was about Jake's trial.

GOOD COP GONE BAD, the headline screamed in block letters. PARTNER TESTIFIES IN POLICE CORRUPTION TRIAL.

My father sighed.

Joe clicked onto the next article: CORRUPT COP CONVICTED!

There were pictures of a big, beefy, brown-haired man being led away in handcuffs. The article described his violent outburst in the courtroom, threatening his former partner, Fenton Hardy. There was a smaller picture of Dad in his uniform, standing in front of the station house.

"Man! You look so young," said Joe. "Look how thick your hair was!"

Dad winced. "Hey, this trip down memory lane is painful enough without comments about my receding hairline."

Joe chuckled and clicked onto the next article. It was dated five years later. There weren't any big headlines or photos, just a couple of paragraphs about Jake Johansen being released from the county jail.

"He only got five years?" I asked Dad.

"Yeah, he was released early. For good behavior, believe it or not."

The next couple of documents were high school portraits of Jake's sons, Fred and Jim.

"Wow. They *do* look a lot like us," I commented. "Except their hair is darker."

"Are you kidding? I'm *much* better looking than him," Joe protested.

"In your dreams, maybe."

"No, in the mirror. You're just jealous, Frank."

"I'm just being honest, Joe," I teased.

Joe's jaw dropped. "Dad, I'm better looking than that guy in the photo, right?"

Our father sighed. "You're *both* better looking, okay? But check it out. The Johansen boys have straight noses and strong chins, just like you two. With a couple of haircuts and a dye job, they could easily pass as Frank and Joe Hardy."

"They wish," Joe muttered, opening the next document.

I shot a glance at Dad. We both snickered.

Another news article filled the screen. The headline read, SAN DIEGO GANG STRIKES AGAIN. The story was a year old and included a long list of local stores that had been robbed.

The next article featured a mug shot of Jake Johansen. He had been charged with burglary but was released because of lack of evidence.

Dad studied the picture carefully. "Look at that. Jake

lost some of his hair too," he said with a smirk. "But he didn't lose that crazy look in his eyes."

The final article was short and sweet: SUSPECTS DISAPPEAR! LOCAL POLICE FAIL TO CATCH THE SAN DIEGO GANG.

Dad sat back in the armchair and started tapping his foot.

Joe clicked off the pocket communicator. "Okay, Dad. What next? Should we set some booby traps in case 'Jake and Sons' pay us another visit?"

Our father was about to respond when his cell phone rang. He pulled it out of his shirt pocket and answered the call.

"Hello. Oh, hi, Bill. Yes. Uh-huh. Sure, I can come down to the station. Yes, I understand. No problem. I can be there in about an hour. Okay. I'll see you there."

Dad clicked off the phone and looked at us.

"Let me guess," I said. "That was your friend Bill from the police force."

Dad nodded. "They want to ask me some questions down at the station. I'm sure they want to find out what I know."

"What are you going to tell them?" I asked.

"I'm not sure," he answered. "This thing might be too dangerous to handle alone. I know Jake. And I know he won't stop until I'm either behind bars or buried in the ground."

"We can catch these guys, Dad," said Joe.

Our father looked at us. "Maybe. But if you guys get hurt . . ."

"We won't," Joe insisted. "Just give us twenty-four hours."

"I don't know, Joe."

"At least think about it on your way to the police station."

Dad agreed—reluctantly. Still, he headed back to his car, advising us to take turns standing guard. "Call me if you see anyone approach the cabin," he said. "And find a good place to hide."

He got into the car and drove off down the dirt road.

"Go get the binoculars," I said to Joe. "We need a good lookout post."

My brother turned and went inside the cabin, while I looked around for a good vantage point. A few seconds later he returned with the binoculars.

"I could climb up on the roof," he said, pointing at the cabin. "I bet I could see the road better."

"Knock yourself out."

Pushing a rusty rain barrel next to the cabin, my brother scrambled up to the rooftop, then looked through the high-powered binoculars.

"This is perfect!" he yelled down at me. "I can see the entrance to the lake from up here. And there's Dad's car, heading down the road. And . . ."

He sucked in his breath.

"What is it?" I shouted. "What do you see?"

"Trouble."

"What?"

"It's the Johansen boys. They're down near the entrance, dragging something out of the woods!"

"What is it?"

"I can't tell. No! Wait! It's a huge log! They're dragging it into the road."

My heart started to sink.

"They're making a roadblock, Frank!"

I couldn't believe what I was hearing.

Our father's driving right into a trap.

"We have to warn him!" I shouted. Of course, my cell was out of juice. I turned to get my motorcycle, but Joe stopped me in my tracks.

"It's too late, Frank!" he yelled. "The boys are hiding in the bushes, and Dad's car just stopped in front of the log!"

I glanced down at the trail, feeling totally helpless.

He's going to be ambushed.

"What's happening now?" I asked.

"Dad is getting out of the car!" Joe yelled back. "He's walking to the log!"

No, Dad! Stop!

Joe's voice grew louder. "The boys are running up behind him! They're holding baseball bats!"

Turn around, Dad! Look out!

"Oh! Man!"

My brother gasped.

"What's happening, Joe?" I shouted up to the roof, dreading the answer.

"They clubbed him in the head! Dad's down!"

11.

The Body in the Trunk

I stared through the binoculars, totally stunned by what I was seeing.

My father lay unmoving on the ground in the middle of the road. Our evil twins stood over him, holding their bats high in the air—preparing to strike again.

"What's happening now?" Frank shouted up at me.

I didn't know what to say.

Dad's not moving.

"Please," I whispered softly. "Be alive, be alive."

"What did you say?" Frank asked me.

I didn't know how to tell my brother that the Johansen boys might have just killed our father.

Then I saw Dad move. His head turned from side to side. The two boys held the bats up threateningly.

"Is Dad okay?" asked Frank. "Is he moving?"

"Yes," I answered back.

I squinted my eyes and saw another figure walk out of the woods.

"Frank! Jake Johansen is there!"

"What's he doing?"

"He's carrying rope! They're tying Dad up!"

I watched in silence as the three criminals bound and gagged our father. Then they started dragging him back to his car.

"They're opening up the trunk of the car," I yelled down to Frank. "They're putting Dad inside and closing it. Now they're getting into the car. Jake's in the driver's seat."

"Come on!" Frank shouted. "We have to catch them before they get away!"

I lowered the binoculars and slid down the angled roof of the cabin. Landing on my feet and rolling in the dirt, I jumped up and followed Frank to our motorcycles. In five seconds flat, we were revved up and ready to go.

We tore off down the road, kicking up dirt behind us.

Swerving left, then right, we skidded around one of the bends—and nearly crashed our bikes.

We're not going to make it, I thought for a moment.

But failure was not an option.

We had to save Dad.

We steadied our bikes and zoomed down the long arching trail that circled the mountain. I glanced down over the side of the road. At first I felt a little dizzy from the plunging view below. Then I spotted Dad's car.

"Frank! Stop!" I yelled, waving my arm.

We squeezed the brakes and stopped. I waved Frank over to the side and pointed down.

"Look! They're turning the car around! They're coming back!"

"We can't let them see us," said Frank.

So we turned around too and started driving back up the mountain. The upward slope was so steep that it slowed us down. I was afraid the Johansens were going plow right into our backsides unless we picked up the pace.

"Joe! This way!"

Frank nodded toward a small dirt path that branched off from the main road. We turned our motorcycles onto the path, pulled them up behind a thick patch of bushes, and killed the engines.

"Duck! Here they come," I said.

My brother and I crouched down and watched our father's car drive by. I could see our evil twins in the back seat. They were playing with the clown wigs we'd left in the car.

Losers.

Once they disappeared up the road, I looked at Frank and asked, "Should we call the cops?"

"Do you have your cell phone with you?"

"No. Do you?"

"Left it back in the cabin."

"Well, that leaves us no choice, Frank," I said, climbing onto my motorcycle. "Let's go help Dad."

Frank shook his head. "Not on our bikes. The engines are too loud. They'd hear us coming. Let's just leave them here and hike back on foot."

"Okay. Let's move."

We figured we could make good time by heading straight up the mountain through the woods, instead of using the main road that zigzagged its way back and forth.

Of course, we didn't think about the steep cliffs we had to climb.

Or the snakes.

"Joe, don't move."

I was about to pull myself up onto a rocky ledge when I heard a low hissing sound. Slowly I turned my head—and found myself face-to-face with a large brown snake.

Frank stood above me on the ledge—and smirked.

"Stop laughing, Frank," I whispered. "Do something."

"Like what? Like this?"

He kicked the snake over the ledge and helped me up. "You don't have to thank me."

"I wasn't planning on it."

Soon we were able to move more quickly, and we

reached the cabin before too long. We crept up behind a large tree and crouched down in the tall grass.

"I don't see them," Frank whispered.

Dad's car was parked out in front—but Jake and his sons were nowhere in sight.

"There they are," I said.

Jake emerged from the cabin. His sons came tromping through the woods out back. "Did you find them?" he asked.

"No," said the older son.

"Should we keep looking?" asked the younger one.

Jake shook his head. "They'll show up sooner or later. Help me carry the squealer inside."

The three of them walked to the car. Jake leaned in over the dashboard and popped the trunk. The boys opened it—and jumped back.

Dad's feet may have been tied, but that didn't stop him from trying to kick his abductors in the face.

"Ouch!" yelped the younger boy. "He got me in the chin!"

"Poor baby," said the older one, laughing. "He might have ruined your profile. Or mussed your hair."

"You're just jealous."

Frank nudged my arm. "They sound like us too," he whispered. "It's eerie."

I shot him a dirty look, then turned back toward the cabin.

Jake was shaking his ham-size fist at his sons. "Stop

joking around, you twerps, and help me pick him up."

The boys stopped laughing and reached into the trunk.

"On the count of three."

"Jim can't count that high."

"You're dead, Fred."

"One, two, *three*!"

Jake and his sons hoisted my father up and out of the trunk.

Dad, of course, put up a good fight.

He squirmed and kicked and bucked like a wild bronco, knocking one of the boys to the ground.

Way to go, Dad!

"Get up, Fred!" Jake yelled. "Hold him tight, Jim! Now move it! Bring him inside!"

Struggling to hold on to their captive, the trio shuffled slowly toward the cabin. Dad twisted and turned and tried to fight them, but it was no use. The rope was wrapped too tightly around his arms and legs.

Finally they reached the doorway. "Feet first, Fred." Jake nodded to his older son.

Poor Fred. He tried his hardest to pull my father through the doorway. But every time he took a step, Dad would kick his foot against the frame so they couldn't carry him through.

"Come on!" Jake bellowed. "Hold his legs! Now pull him through! Pull!"

Dad wedged his foot against the door frame again. Fred howled in frustration.

"This is like watching the Three Stooges," I whispered to Frank.

Finally, after the fourth or fifth attempt to carry my father inside, Jake came up with another plan.

"Head first," he announced to his sons. "Okay, Jim. You swing around to your left. No, stupid! Your *other* left!"

I had to cover my mouth to keep from laughing out loud.

The terrible trio managed to get my father halfway through the doorway. But then, at the last minute, Dad hooked the tops of his feet on the edge of the door frame. They pulled and pulled, but my father wouldn't let go.

"Okay, boys," said Jake. "On the count of three, I want you to pull as hard as you can. One, two, *three!*"

They pulled. Dad unhooked his feet. And all of them went flying backward into the cabin.

CRASH!

It sounded like a clap of thunder when they hit the floor.

"Stupid!"

I glanced at Frank. "We can take these guys."

My brother frowned. "Don't be so sure. They managed to knock us down in the jewelry store. Or have you forgotten about being trapped under that display case?"

"Give me a break." I turned my attention back to the cabin. I could hear a scuffle going on inside but couldn't see anything. "Do you think they're going to come out and look for us again?"

"I wouldn't doubt it," said Frank. "I'm sure the younger one is dying to know how you get your hair so soft and shiny."

"This isn't the time for jokes, Frank."

He sat back in the grass. "Maybe it is."

"What do you mean?"

"I think we should wait a few minutes before trying to save Dad. The sun's going down, and it'll be dark soon."

"Okay, genius. How are we going to get Dad out of there?" I asked, glancing at the cabin. "Have you come up with some sort of brilliant master plan?"

"Not really. Have you?"

"Hmmm. Let me think."

"Don't hurt yourself, Joe."

"I got it," I said. "I'll sneak up to the cabin and climb onto the roof. You stay here in the woods and throw stones to create a distraction. Then, when the boys come out to look for us, I'll jump down from the roof and untie Dad."

Frank tilted his head. "Not bad. But what if Big Jake is guarding the doorway?"

I shrugged. "I'll jump on his back and bite his ear."

Frank studied the cabin for a minute, then shrugged his shoulders. "It could work."

I couldn't believe my ears. "Really? You think it's a good idea?"

"Sure, bro."

"You think it's a brilliant master plan?"

"Don't push it."

As soon as the sun went down, we got ourselves into position. Frank gathered a bunch of palm-size rocks and found a good hiding place beneath a fallen tree. Me, I got down on the ground and crept up slowly toward the rain barrel next to the cabin.

Don't blow it, Joe, I told myself.

I lifted one foot gently onto the barrel and stepped up, grabbing the edge of the roof with my hands. Then slowly and carefully, I pulled my whole body up.

Rrrrk.

The roof creaked a little beneath my weight. I froze—and waited. I expected Jake and his sons to come rushing outside any second. But nothing happened.

Working my way toward the front entrance of the cabin, I crouched down and got into position.

Then I waved at Frank.

Okay. Let's do this.

In the darkness, I saw my brother's arm swing through the air. A rock went flying into the bushes near the cabin.

WHACK!

Bull's-eye.

The leaves rustled for a few seconds. Then Frank threw another rock.

WHACK!

It didn't take long for Jake and his sons to open the door and come running outside. I glanced down at the top of their heads—and noticed that Jake had lost a *lot* more hair than my dad had.

I shook the thought from my head and tried to concentrate.

Should I jump him now?

No, his sons were right next to him. Three to one are lousy odds.

WHACK!

I heard another rock hit a nearby tree branch. Fred and Jim turned their heads and squinted. "It came from over there," said Fred. "Should we go check it out, Dad?"

"No," said Jake. "We'll make them come to us."

I didn't know what he was talking about. But it didn't matter. I was ready for anything.

Or so I thought.

"Frank and Joe Hardy! I know you're out there!" Jake yelled into the darkness. "Now here's what we're going to do. On the count of three, I want you both to come out with your hands up."

Yeah, right, I thought. *Not in a million years, buddy.*

Then he said something that changed my mind.

"If you don't do what I say, I'm going to kill your father."

12.

Countdown to Death

I had to give it to Jake. He was smarter than he looked.

"Fred, go inside and stick your knife against that squealer's neck," he said. "Then wait for my signal."

That was enough to make my skin crawl.

Fred went into the cabin, and Jake took a few steps forward. He was too far away for Joe to jump him—which wasn't such a good idea anyway, since his son was holding a knife to our father's throat.

"Okay, boys, are you ready?" Jake shouted toward the woods. "I'm starting the countdown now."

I took a deep breath.

"One!"

I stood up and started walking toward the cabin. Jake saw me—but he kept counting.

"Two!"

I glanced up at the roof. "Joe! Come on down!"

Jake squinted his eyes and stared at me. He seemed

109

to think I was bluffing, because he opened his mouth to shout out the final—and fatal—number.

"Thr . . ."

Joe jumped down from the roof. Jake spun around and stared at him for a moment. Then a big, ugly smile spread across his face.

"Good boys," he snarled. "You just saved your father's life. Or maybe not. Why don't we all step inside so we can talk about it?"

He waved his arm toward the door. I glanced at Joe and sighed. We didn't have much of a choice—so we turned and headed into the cabin.

WHUMP!

Something hard smashed into the back of my head.

Then everything went black.

I opened my eyes and groaned.

Man! That hurt!

My head felt like it was going to explode. I tried to reach up to see if I was bleeding—but quickly discovered that I couldn't move my arms.

I was tied to a chair.

I looked up and saw Dad and Joe. They were also tied to chairs.

Of course.

We were arranged in a small circle, facing each other. When my eyes met my brother's, I could tell we were thinking the same thing.

We should have seen it coming.

Yep. We should have known that Jake's sons would be waiting for us on opposite sides of the doorway. We should have known they'd be holding baseball bats.

We should have seen it coming.

And now here we were—knocked down, tied up, and out of luck.

"Heads up," Jake growled. He came straight at us wielding a huge square object like some sort of weapon. It took me a second to realize it was the card table.

BAM!

He slammed the table down legs-first on the floor, right in the middle of the three of us. Then he pulled up a chair and sat down, drumming his fingers on the tabletop.

"What's going on, Jake?" asked my father. "I'm not in the mood to play games."

"You're not? Too bad!" the big man shot back. "Because I'm *dying* to playing a few games with the Hardy family. *Mind* games."

"Leave the boys out of this, Jake."

"*Shut up*, Fenton! This is *my* game, and we'll play by *my* rules." He slammed his fist down. "Now let's put our cards on the table."

He pulled a switchblade out of his back pocket and flipped it open.

"I'll go first," said Jake. He spread his left hand

palm-down on the table. Then with his right hand, he began stabbing the knifepoint into the spaces between his fingers.

Tap, tap, tap, tap.

Jake stopped for a second and glared at my father. His face started turning red—and then he exploded.

"You ruined my life, Fenton!"

Jake's deep, booming voice seemed to shake the whole cabin. Everybody froze, even Jake's sons. The tension was so thick, you could cut it with a knife—no pun intended.

After a long, excruciating pause, Jake started tapping with the knife again.

"You were my partner, Fenton. You were my *best friend*. I went to the hospital with you when Frank and Joe were born. I babysat them so you and your wife could have a night on the town. I bought you a new fishing pole for your birthday."

He stopped tapping.

"*Why*, Fenton?" he asked, his voice just a whisper. "*Why* did you turn me in?" His cold, dark eyes zeroed in on my father.

Dad stared back without flinching. "You know why, Jake. You weren't just stealing. You were taking bribes from criminals. You betrayed the police department. You betrayed your family. You betrayed yourself. And you betrayed me, too."

Jake took a deep breath—then started laughing.

"Look who's talking. *You turned me in, Fenton! You testi-fied against me!*"

He stood up quickly, knocking his chair to the floor. Then he started pacing back and forth, mumbling and cursing.

"Do you know what it's like, Fenton? Do have know what it's like to be accused and handcuffed and stripped of your badge and gun? Do you know what it's like to hear your best friend condemn you in a court of law, to have your name dragged through the dirt, to be taken away from your wife and kids? *Do you know what it's like?*"

He buried his face in his hands.

"Tell me," my father said softly. "What's it like, Jake?"

Slowly the big man lowered his hands. His face was red and streaked with tears.

"It's like nothing you could ever imagine," he said. "It's like there's something growing inside you, some-thing dark and powerful. It makes you do terrible things. It makes you lie and cheat and steal. It makes you raise your children for one thing and one thing alone—revenge."

He walked to the window and stared outside.

"I thought by framing your sons for those rob-beries, I could give you a little taste of what I've been going through. But I was wrong. You'll never under-stand what it's like . . . to be me."

I glanced over at Joe. He looked as scared as I did. We were both shaking in our seats. And who could blame us?

We were trapped in a cabin with a madman!

Jake's sons got up and walked over to their father. Fred put his hand on his father's shoulder. "It's going to be okay, Dad. Tonight's the night. You're going to get your revenge."

"Yeah, Dad," said Jim. "It's going to be sweet."

Jake nodded. "You're right, boys. I've waited a long time for this."

He turned around slowly and faced us. There were no more tears in his eyes. There was something else instead, something cold and mean and hateful.

Raising his switchblade, he approached the table. "Do you believe in justice, Fenton?"

My father frowned. "Of course I do, Jake."

"Of course you do. And do you believe that the punishment should fit the crime?"

Dad cleared his throat. "Um, yes."

"Okay, then," said Jake, picking up the chair and sitting down at the table. "So how would you punish a man who destroys your life?"

My stomach churned. I knew the answer he was looking for.

You destroy his life.

My father didn't say anything at first. I could see his mind racing, trying to think of a way to respond to Jake's twisted logic.

Finally he turned his head and looked Jake in the eye. "What do you want from me, Jake?" he said calmly. "I can't change something that happened sixteen years ago. It's all in the past. There's nothing I can do to take it back."

Jake smiled that crazy smile of his. "Yes, there is, Fenton. There *is* something you can do."

He stood up and walked to the kitchen counter. He picked up a notebook and a pen, then brought them over and laid them on the table in front of my father.

"You can write a confession," he said.

Dad looked up, a little surprised by the strange request. "Um, what do you want me to confess?"

"All of your crimes," said Jake. "I'll tell you what to write. Then, when I'm finished, you can sign it."

My father stared down at the notebook and pen. "Okay, sure. Are you going to untie me, or do you expect me to write with the pen in my mouth?"

Jake let out a little laugh. "Fred, untie Mr. Hardy's right hand."

The boy bent over to loosen the knots. My father and I exchanged a brief glance. We both knew that Jake was taking a big risk by doing this.

This could be our only chance to get out of this mess.

Once untied, Dad raised his free arm slowly and reached for the pen. Jake took a step backward and told my father to write down everything he said.

"I, Fenton Hardy, hereby confess to the following

crimes. I am guilty of framing my partner on the police force, Jake Johansen. I wrongly accused him of theft, bribery, and corruption. He is an innocent man, and I apologize to him and his family for the pain I have caused them."

My father wrote it all down, word for word. Jake continued.

"The guilt has been eating away at me for years. I do not deserve the awards and citations I received as a police detective. I do not deserve to have sons like Frank and Joe, who robbed a bank, stole jewelry, and held up stores just to please their father. *I do not deserve to live.*"

My father hesitated when he got to the last sentence.

"Write it down!" Jake bellowed. "Now sign it!"

My father signed the confession. Jake looked over his shoulder while he did it.

Then, with lightning speed, Dad's arm jerked back, jabbing Jake in the gut with his elbow. Grasping the pen like a weapon, he swung his arm around.

Get him, Dad!

But Jake was too fast for him. His beefy arms clamped around my father like a giant vise, pinning his free hand to his side. The pen dropped to the floor.

Jake barked at his sons. "Jim! Fred! Tie his arm! Hurry!"

I looked over at Joe. He looked ticked. And a little nervous.

When Fred and Jim finished tying up my father's arm, Jake patted Dad's cheek with his palm.

"Nice try, Fenton. Too bad it didn't work."

My father fumed. "Okay, Jake. You got your confession. What more do you want from me?"

Jake stood up and laughed. "What more do I want? That's a very good question. The answer is simple."

He pulled my father's head back.

"I want to kill you."

He raised the knife.

13.
Cabin Fever

He's going to do it. He's going to kill my dad.

The blade flashed before my eyes. A beam of light flickered across my father's face as Jake lowered the knife to his throat.

No!

I struggled against the ropes that bound me to the chair. But it was no use. There was nothing I could do.

"Take a good look at your sons, Fenton," Jake snarled. "It's the last time you'll ever see them."

His fingers tightened around the handle of the switchblade.

"Don't do it, Jake!" I screamed.

"Stop!" said Frank. "Please!"

He looked at us and laughed.

"Watch closely, boys," Jake sneered. "This is what happens to dirty rotten squealers."

The knife twitched in his grasp.

"Dad, wait," said Jim, peering out the window. "Someone's coming. A car just pulled up."

Jake lowered his arm that was around my father's neck. He rushed over to the window and peeked through the curtains. "Who are they? What are they doing here?" He looked at us as if we knew.

Your guess is as good as mine.

I glanced at Dad and Frank. They looked as puzzled as I was.

We heard an engine rumbling outside. Suddenly it stopped, then two car doors opened and closed. I could make out the sound of footsteps approaching. There was a knock at the door.

Jake waved at his sons and pointed at the baseball bats lying on the floor. Fred and Jim picked them up and waited by the door.

The people outside knocked again. And again.

Then someone shouted, "Hey! You guys!"

I groaned when I recognized the voice.

"It's us! Chet and Belinda! Let us in!"

Jake turned off the lights and opened the door.

I couldn't see what happened next—but I could hear it.

First Belinda walked in and said, "What's up with the lights, guys? I can't see a thing."

Chet whispered in a goofy ghost voice, "Ewww, scary."

Then I heard a lot of banging and crashing and

screaming—followed by the sounds of two loud thumps on the floor.

I wasn't sure what happened. But it didn't sound good. Especially when a deep voice broke the silence.

"Good work, boys. Now tie them up."

When the lights were turned on, I saw Chet sitting across from me at the card table. He was tied securely to the fourth chair—and obviously annoyed.

"Who are these guys?" he asked.

"Our evil twins," I told him.

"*These* are your evil twins?" said a voice next to the sofa.

I looked over to see Belinda on the floor, being tied up by Fred and Jim.

"They *can't* be your evil twins," she said. "You're *much* better looking."

I glanced at Frank. "I told you so."

My brother rolled his eyes and shook his head.

"Shut up! All of you!" Jake yelled from the kitchen. He hunched over the stove and peered into the oven.

"Are you planning to cook something?" I asked.

He looked up and sneered at me. "Yeah, kid. I'm hungry . . . for *revenge*."

Fred and Jim finished tying up Belinda. As soon as they were done, they stood up and joined their father in the kitchen.

"We tied up their friends, Dad," said Jim.

"Good," he snarled. "Any friend of the Hardys is an enemy of mine."

"What are you planning to do?" asked Fred.

"I'll tell you in a minute. Look and see if you can find a candle around here."

A candle?

What was he planning to do? Cook us a romantic candlelight dinner?

Yeah, right.

He was probably going to cook *us*.

Fred and Jim started searching through the kitchen drawers and cupboards. Jake walked over to us, leaned over the card table, and picked up Dad's signed confession. His cold, dark eyes scanned the paper—and an evil grin flashed across his face.

"So what are you planning to do with that, Jake?" asked my father.

Jake glared back at him. "I'm going to send it to every newspaper in the country. I'm going to tell everyone the truth about Fenton Hardy and his little trained monkeys, Frank and Joe."

"Nobody will believe it," said Dad.

"They will," said Jake. "They'll believe every word of it . . . once they find your dead body."

My father didn't say anything.

"Remember the last sentence of your confession, Fenton? You wrote, and I quote, 'I do not deserve to live.'"

Dad took a deep breath and let it out slowly.

"Everyone will think you killed yourself," said Jake. "And you took a few others along with you."

My father's head snapped up. "Leave the kids out of this, Jake. I'm the one you want. Go ahead and kill me. But let the others go."

Jake chuckled softly and started pacing back and forth. "That would be nice of me, wouldn't it? But you're forgetting something, Fenton." He stopped and turned. "I'm not a nice guy."

No kidding, I thought.

Jake looked at Dad's confession again. Then he tore the page out of the notebook, folded it carefully, and stuffed it into his back pocket. "I've been dreaming of this day," he muttered.

I looked at Chet. His mouth was hanging open, his face frozen with fear. Then I glanced over at Belinda lying on the floor. She was trembling.

Why did we let them come here?

I felt horrible about it. Frank was right. We shouldn't have allowed them to get involved.

"Hey, Dad! I found a candle!"

Fred walked over and handed the candle to his father. It was one of those short, stubby ones—I think they call them votives. Jake took the candle and set it on the mantel above the fireplace.

"It's not much of a candle, but it'll do the job," he said, turning back to us. "But with a fancy cabin like this, you don't really need candles, do you, Fenton? This place is fully equipped with all the modern conveniences. Electric lights. A shower. A toilet." He paused. "And this wonderful gas stove over here."

Jake crossed the room to the kitchen.

"I see that you installed a big gas tank for this," he continued. "That must have been expensive. But hey, you only live once, right? And gas ranges are so much better than electric, aren't they?"

I didn't like the playful tone of his voice. It was even creepier than when he was yelling.

"There's just one problem with gas stoves," said Jake. He opened the oven door and lifted up the stovetop. "Sometimes the pilot lights go out."

Don't do it, I thought.

He leaned over and blew out all of the little blue flames.

The he turned all of the knobs.

Sssssssssss.

The gas started hissing from the stove.

"Do you hear that?" asked Jake. He closed his eyes and took a deep breath. "Do you smell that? No? Well, give it time. In just a few minutes, the whole cabin will be filled with gas."

He walked back into the living room. Digging through his pockets, he pulled out a pack of matches. Then he strolled toward the fireplace.

"Did you realize that most accidents occur in the

home?" he asked us. "Candles, for instance, can be very, very dangerous. If a candle falls over, it could set fire to the curtains—and burn down the whole house. Or if there's a gas leak, it could set off a major explosion."

I tensed up in my chair.

He's going to blow us up.

Jake leaned back and chortled. The sound of his laughter made me sick to my stomach.

Or maybe it was the gas.

Glancing nervously at the kitchen, I listened to the sharp hissing of the open valves.

Sssssssssss.

I could smell it, too. It made me feel queasy.

"Make sure the windows are closed, boys," Jake said to his sons. He opened the pack of matches and pulled one out. Just as he was about to light it, Fred yelled something in a panicked voice.

"Dad! It's the cops!"

Suddenly a loud siren blared outside. A flashing red light flickered through the window and lit up the walls inside the cabin. Then a loud voice echoed through a megaphone.

"THIS IS THE POLICE. WE KNOW YOU'RE IN THERE."

Jake was stunned. He looked at Fred, then Jim, with wide-open eyes and said, "We have to get out of here!" He turned his head back and forth, searching desperately for a way to escape. "Quick! The back door!"

The two boys flung open the door and dashed out. Jake was right behind them.

I let out a big sigh of relief.

They're gone.

The loud wail of a police siren had never sounded better. I was so happy at that moment I didn't even mind the odor of the gas.

Just relax and wait for the police, I told myself. *First they'll turn off the gas. Then they'll untie us. And then they'll go catch the bad guys.*

I looked at my family and friends and started to smile. "We're going to make it, guys," I said.

But then Jake reappeared in the doorway.

"Oops, I almost forgot something."

He ran back to the mantel, struck a match, and lit the candle.

POLICE BULLETIN

June 15, 9:35 p.m.
RED ALERT

ATTENTION: all patrol cars. We need backup at Lake Midnight just north of the highway. Take the dirt road to the last cabin on the right. Earlier today, two boys in clown outfits were seen getting out of a car, which we followed to this location. We believe it could be the Hardy gang's hideout.

Two of our officers are now approaching the cabin. We could definitely use some backup here. Please send all available squad cars.

The criminals may be armed and dangerous.

Proceed with caution.

Over and out.

14.

Totally Barbecued

Okay, Jake. You're evil. We get it.

You didn't have to light the candle to prove it.

I stared at the flickering flame on the mantel—and listened to the hissing stove in the kitchen. The whole cabin was starting to stink like gas.

I have to admit I was a little surprised that Jake risked blowing himself up to get his revenge. But then I remembered something.

The guy is totally bonkers.

"Aw, don't look so sad," said Jake, seeing our faces. "You've all lived good clean wholesome lives. You deserve to go out *with a bang.*"

He turned and ran out the back door of the cabin. Unfortunately, he remembered to close it behind him.

We were sealed in.

With a leaking gas stove. And an open flame.

"Don't worry," said Dad. "The police will come and untie us before the gas tank blows."

Everybody seemed a little relieved—until we heard the police officers' voices outside.

"Look!" one of them shouted. "Somebody's running behind the cabin!"

"Go after him!" said another. "I'll stay here and smoke out the others!"

A pair of footsteps charged off into the woods. Then we heard the loud screech of a megaphone.

"WE HAVE YOU SURROUNDED. COME OUT WITH YOUR HANDS UP."

I glanced at my father. "Are you *sure* they're going to save us?"

Dad hesitated at first. Then he said, "I'm sure. They'll probably bust the door down any second now."

I wasn't convinced.

We waited. And waited. But nothing happened.

A minute later we heard the voice on the megaphone again. "IT WON'T DO YOU ANY GOOD TO STAY INSIDE. WE CAN WAIT HERE ALL NIGHT."

"Oh, man, we're dead," said Joe, groaning. "We're going to be totally barbecued."

Chet let out a little whimper, and Belinda started to cry.

Good job, Joe.

I glared at my brother. "If my feet weren't tied, I'd kick you in the shin."

"Okay, stay calm, everyone," said Dad. "Maybe if we all scream for help, the police will hear us and know we're in trouble."

It seemed like a good idea.

"Okay, on the count of three," he said.

"Skip it," I interrupted. "Let's just scream."

We turned our heads to the door and shouted as loud as we could.

"HELP! HELP!! HELP!!! *HELP!!!*"

Thirty seconds later we stopped to listen for the cops' reaction.

Nothing.

All we could hear was the hissing of the stove.

Sssssssssss!

We tried it again, screaming at the top of our lungs. No luck. The police didn't seem to hear us at all.

"COME OUT WITH YOUR HANDS UP!"

Chet looked at us across the table and asked in a frightened voice, "So does anyone have a Plan B?"

Nobody said anything. But believe me, we were racking our brains. Our lives depended on it.

Okay, so we're tied up.

Again.

I thought about what happened at the Vehicle Park the other morning. Then it hit me.

"Joe! Do you still have that pocketknife in your

shoe? I mean, the one you had in your boot the other day?"

My brother's eyes lit up. "Yes!" Then he frowned. "But I can't reach it. My hands are tied to the back legs of the chair, and my ankles are tied to the front legs."

I tried to think. My eyes gazed across the room while my mind searched for an answer.

"I got it," I said. "Belinda! Do you think you can shimmy across the floor and grab Joe's shoe?"

Belinda blinked her eyes sleepily. "I'm feeling a little woozy from the gas," she said. "But for you, Frank, I can shimmy all the way to Hollywood."

She winked at me—which caught me totally off guard. I mean, come on. Even in the face of death, she was flirting.

Deal with it, Frank, I told myself. *Even in the face of death, you're blushing.*

Without any further discussion, Belinda started to wriggle and squirm across the cabin floor. Within seconds she had shimmied under the card table and next to Joe's chair.

Impressive.

"Which shoe?" she asked.

"The right one," Joe answered.

Belinda rolled over and pressed her back against Joe's right shoe. Then she tried to reach up with her hands.

"Can't reach inside," she said.

"Joe," I said. "Do you think you can knock yourself to the floor?"

"You'd like that, wouldn't you?"

"Joe!"

"I'll do it! I'll do it!"

He started rocking back and forth, side to side, faster and faster, until—*WHAM*—he crashed to the floor right next to Belinda.

"Ow! My shoulder!" he cried out.

Belinda didn't waste any time. She shimmied into position and wiggled her fingers into his shoe. "I got it!" she cheered. "Now what do I do?"

"Hand it to me," said Joe, shooting me a playful look. "I've done this before."

"Here you go," said Belinda, handing off the knife.

My brother's face tensed up as he worked the blade behind his back, slowly cutting the rope that bound his wrists.

"Hurry, Joe," I whispered. "We're counting on you."

"Just another minute," he said, sawing back and forth.

I listened to the hissing stove—and smelled the leaking gas. Chet looked like he was about to pass out. Come to think of it, I didn't feel so great myself.

We might not have another minute, I thought.

"Just one more . . . Got it!" Joe shouted, pulling his arm free and raising his hand in the air.

131

"Quick! Untie yourself!" I yelled.

He reached behind his chair and started unknotting his other hand. As fast he could, he ripped the ropes away from his body, then grabbed the knife and cut his feet free.

"Go, Joe!" Belinda shouted.

My brother jumped to his feet.

"Blow out the candle!" said Dad. "Then open the doors and turn off the stove!"

My brother followed my father's orders as if he were a contestant on a reality show, racing through a bunch of crazy stunts to win a million dollars.

In this case, however, the prize was staying alive.

First Joe ran to the fireplace and blew out the candle. Then he dashed to the back door and flung it open. Spinning around, he charged across the cabin, hopped over Belinda, and opened the front door. Finally, he sprinted to the kitchen and turned all the knobs, one by one.

Sssssssssssss . . .

The hissing stopped. A warm evening breeze drifted in through the open doorways. Everybody took a deep breath.

Ahhh. Fresh air.

Joe leaned over the kitchen counter, panting. "I suppose you all want me to untie you now," he said.

"Ladies first," said Belinda.

As Joe crouched down to untie her, I turned my

head to look through the front doorway. I thought I saw something move outside, but it was hard to tell with the flashing red police lights shining in my eyes.

Suddenly a policeman jumped into the cabin—with his gun pointed right at us.

"Freeze!"

Chet scoffed. "Does it look like we're going anywhere, officer?"

The cop squinted and stared, but he didn't lower his gun.

Dad took over from there. "Excuse me, officer," he said in a calm voice. "I'm former police detective Fenton Hardy. These are my sons and their friends. And I guarantee you—despite the looks of my boys—we are *not* the criminals you're looking for."

The officer didn't seem convinced. "What did you say your name was?"

"Fenton Hardy."

"Fenton? Is that you?" The policeman lowered his gun. "I'm Wally Stern. You probably don't remember me, but I was a rookie during your last year on the force. Wow. Fenton Hardy. You were one heck of a detective. Sorry I didn't recognize you. You lost a lot of hair."

Dad winced. "Yeah, and you put on a lot of weight."

The officer laughed and patted his belly. "Too many donuts," he said. "So do you guys need a hand getting untied?"

I thought he'd never ask.

"Thanks, Wally," said Dad. "I appreciate it."

Officer Stern leaned over and started undoing the knots around my father's wrists. The two of them started chatting about other guys on the police force.

I glanced down at Joe, who was still on the floor trying to cut through Belinda's knots. "Psst, Joe," I whispered. "Untie me first."

Joe nodded like he understood. Then he got up and started slicing my ropes.

"What about ladies first?" asked Belinda.

"Frank has a date," Joe told her.

"With whom?"

"His evil twin."

"Oh." She nodded and winked.

As soon as Dad and I were free, Officer Stern squatted down to untie Belinda. "Easy," she told him. "The ropes are cutting into my skin. I'm *very* sensitive, so you have to untie the knots slowly. *Ouch!* I said *slowly*."

She was giving us more time. *Nice!*

Moving quickly, I tiptoed across the room, grabbed my backpack, and signaled to my father and brother. One after the other, we slipped out the back door.

"Follow me," said Dad, leading us around the side of the cabin. "Check it out. There's only one squad car out front. I'm sure they asked for backup, but Jake and his sons will probably be long gone by the time they show up."

"What about Wally's partner?" I asked. "We heard him go after Jake."

Dad rolled his eyes. "If he's anything like Wally, he's probably lost in the woods right now."

"Or eating donuts," said Joe.

Dad sighed. "I really don't want to let Jake get away. He'll just come after us again."

"Let's go," said Joe.

We hurried past the flashing police lights and plunged into the darkness of the woods. We headed toward the hiking trail around the lake—we figured they'd stay away from the main road. At first we kept tripping over rocks and branches. But once our eyes adjusted to the moonlight, we were able to pick up the pace.

"We could use the night-vision goggles," I suggested.

Dad and Joe stopped and looked at me. "You have them with you?" asked my father.

"Yeah. That's why I grabbed my backpack on the way out."

"Are mine in there too?" asked Joe.

"Yup."

"You think of everything, Frank."

"Somebody has to."

I crouched down next to a tree, opened the backpack, and pulled out a pair of night goggles. I was about to hand them to Joe when I heard something.

It was a grunting sound.

Up in the tree.

Right over our heads.

Dad and Joe heard it too. Slowly the three of us raised our heads and looked up.

It was Jake.

Sitting on a large branch, he glared down at us and laughed that horrible laugh.

"Hello, Hardys."

He let out a loud roar, like some sort of wild animal.

Then he leaped from the tree and tackled my father to the ground.

15.
Cliffhanger

WHAM!

Jake's body slammed down so hard and fast that Dad didn't even know what hit him. The two men rolled across the ground, their arms swinging and legs kicking.

Get him, Dad!

But Jake was definitely bigger and stronger. With a single thrust, he pinned my father down in the dirt, then started punching. "You're dead, Hardy!"

Frank and I couldn't just stand there watching our dad get beaten to a pulp.

So we joined the fight.

"AUUUUGHHH!!!"

I ran and leaped on top of Jake's back, swinging my fists and digging my knees into his ribs. Frank grabbed him around the neck and tried to put him in a head-lock.

"Get *off*!" Jake howled.

I swear the guy was like the Incredible Hulk. His whole body just exploded, his arms pumping up and shooting out like two battering rams.

Frank and I went flying through the air.

"Oof!"

I landed with a heavy thud against the trunk of a tree, banging my head against the bark.

"Oww!"

Frank crashed on top of me a second later.

A little stunned, we lifted our heads and saw Jake running into the woods—and our father chasing after him.

"We have to help Dad," I said, giving Frank a little shove. "Get up."

By the time both of us got to our feet, Jake and Dad were nowhere in sight. "Where did they go?" I said.

Frank bent down and picked up the night-vision goggles lying next to the tree. Peering through the eyepiece, he quickly scanned the woods. "I don't see them."

"Maybe the view's better by the lake," I said. "Come on. Let's go."

We started jogging along the trail until we reached the edge of Lake Midnight. The surface of the water was calm and smooth, like a polished sheet of glass, and it reflected the bright white moon in the sky. Frank climbed up onto one of the lifeguard chairs and looked around.

"Do you see Jake and Dad?" I asked.

He adjusted the night-vision goggles. "No, but I think I found Fred and Jim."

"Where?"

"Over there, about two hundred yards away." He pointed toward the base of Pinewood Peak.

"Why would they go that way? It's a dead end."

Pinewood Peak was a giant stone tower that could only be climbed from the other side of the lake. You couldn't reach the trail from this direction. So Fred and Jim were about to walk right into a solid wall of rock.

"Do you want to go after them?" asked Frank.

"Do bears poop in the woods?" I asked.

My brother hopped down from the lifeguard chair, and we headed off toward Pinewood Peak. Running as fast as we could, we thought we'd be able to sneak up behind them and launch a surprise attack.

But we thought wrong.

"Where did they go?" I asked when we reached the base of the rocky peak.

Frank pulled out the night-vision goggles and made a full scan of the area. "This doesn't make sense. They couldn't have just vanished."

Then he tilted the goggles upward.

"No, wait. There they are."

I looked up and studied the rocky face of Pinewood Peak. There they were, scrambling up the sloping cliff like a pair of professional rock climbers.

Frank nudged my arm. "Are you game?"

"Are you kidding?"

We raced toward the rock wall and started climbing. It was pretty easy at first. The slope wasn't too steep, and the jagged terrain offered plenty of good footholds. Then, after climbing about fifty feet, the going got tough.

No sweat, I told myself. *If they can do it, we can do it.*

I started to wonder if I was kidding myself when my foot slipped off a ledge and I was left dangling over the edge. With both hands I pulled myself up, swinging my legs until my foot hooked onto a jutting rock.

"You okay?" My brother stood six feet above me.

"No . . . problem . . ." I said, huffing and straining.

Finally I managed to flop up onto the ledge. Twisting my head upward, I looked to see our evil twins silhouetted in the moonlight. They were about sixty feet above us.

"Hurry up," Frank whispered. "If they reach the top before we do, we might lose them."

I didn't say anything. Instead I started climbing like a maniac, passing my brother on my way to the top. "Are you coming, Frank?" I asked.

"Show-off," he muttered, scampering after me.

Soon we were gaining on them. Fifty feet, forty feet, thirty feet.

But then something happened.

Frank slipped and banged his knee against a rock.

"*Owww!*"

His voice echoed across the lake. I held my breath for a second, then glanced up.

Oh, great.

Fred and Jim had stopped climbing. And they were looking right at us.

"Frank! They spotted us!"

He didn't have to hear it from me—because a shower of rocks came flying down on us from above.

"Look out!"

I pressed my body against the cliff and covered my head.

Whack!

A stone bounced off my shoulder, followed by another, and another. Just as I thought the rock storm was over, I lifted my head and looked up.

A big rock, about the size of a softball, sailed down toward my head. I ducked down and . . .

Whack!

It hit Frank in the arm—and knocked him off the ledge.

"Auugh!"

Frank howled the whole way down, sliding and bumping over the rocky cliff until—*whump*—he landed on another ledge.

I started climbing down to help him. "Frank! Are you okay?"

He raised his head slowly and looked at me. "Keep going, Joe! Don't let them get away!"

"But Frank!"

"Don't worry, man," he said, standing up and brushing himself off. "I'm right behind you."

I turned back and looked up the side of the cliff. Fred and Jim were climbing faster now. They'd reach the top in a matter of minutes—unless I could stop them somehow.

I reached up and grabbed the side of the cliff. A piece of rock broke away in my hand.

Yes! Ammunition!

Gazing up, I set my sights on Jim—the one with the lame dyed hair—and I threw the rock as hard as I could.

Whack!

"Owww!"

Bull's-eye.

The guy staggered and slipped. Then he started sliding down the face of the cliff, his hands and feet flailing. Finally he skidded to a stop on a small ledge. Catching his breath, he peeked over the edge and glared at me.

"You're going down, Hardy!"

I could tell he was searching for loose rocks to throw. So I scrambled to a hiding place under a jutting rock and reached for another stone.

Jim threw his first—but he missed.

I leaned out, looked up, and zeroed in on his older brother, Fred. I hurled my stone.

Whack!

It hit him in the hand.

Nice shot, Joe, I complimented myself. *You're two for two.*

Fred went sliding down the cliff. He tried really hard to stop his fall by digging in his feet and grasping for something to hold on to. Unfortunately, he grabbed onto his younger brother.

"Whooooahh!"

The two of them collided and rolled—right over the ledge.

"AUUUGHHH!"

They started sliding right toward me.

I ducked beneath the jutting rock. If they were going to fall off the cliff, I didn't want to be taken along for the ride. So I hunched down and waited.

Nothing happened.

Then, a few moments later, I heard Fred's voice. He must have slid to a stop about twenty feet above me.

"Don't just sit there, stupid! Help me!"

"Help yourself, stupid!" Jim snapped back.

"Who are you calling stupid?"

"The stupid guy who needs my help, *that's* who!"

Their voices got louder and louder as the argument continued.

I looked down and saw Frank crawling up the cliff toward me. When he reached my hiding spot, he squatted down beside me and pointed up at the Johansen boys.

"Have you ever heard two brothers bicker so much?" he whispered.

"Never," I said. "It's shameful."

Frank stifled a laugh, then gave me a nudge. "Come on. While those two are fighting, let's do some rock climbing. I bet we can beat them to the top."

"I bet I can beat *you* to the top," I said.

The race was on.

Frank and I scurried up the rocks like a pair of mountain goats. We didn't go straight up, because we didn't want to run into Fred and Jim. Instead, we moved at an angle until we were just ten feet away from them.

Believe it or not, Fred and Jim were still fighting.

"If *I'm* stupid, then *you're* super stupid!"

"Oh, yeah? Well, if I'm *super* stupid, then you're *mega* super stupid!"

"Oh, yeah? Well, if I'm . . ."

Suddenly the shouting stopped.

What happened? Did they fall off the ledge?

I turned my head to look. And guess what? My evil double was looking right back at me!

"Hello, stupid," I said.

Jim's jaw dropped open. Fred crawled up on the ledge and poked him in the ribs. "Stop staring. Move it, stupid!" Then the brothers started climbing at full speed.

Frank and I started climbing faster too, but the cliff

was too smooth and steep. We needed to move over to the left and follow behind Fred and Jim.

They're going to beat us to the top.

I hated the idea of those two freaks getting away. Just the thought of it gave me an extra burst of energy. So I took a deep breath and started clawing my way to the top.

"Go get 'em, bro," said Frank as I climbed past him.

I looked up. My evil twin's ankle was just a few feet over my head. I lunged with my right arm, reached up to grab him . . . *and missed*.

"Ha!" Jim screeched, kicking a stone in my face.

It grazed the side of my head, knocking me down a few feet. The blow must have stunned me a little, because I almost lost my grip on the rocks.

Hold on, Joe, I told myself. *Don't give up now.*

After a few deep breaths, I was ready to go. But when I looked up again, Fred and Jim were gone.

They made it. They made it to the top of Pinewood Peak.

I still wasn't ready to give up. Reaching out with my arms, I grabbed the next ledge and hauled myself up. Then I started climbing again, moving faster and faster until . . .

I made it!

My body flopped forward onto the flat surface of the peak. I tried to stand up as fast as I could—even though I knew that Fred and Jim were probably halfway down the hiking trail by now.

But I was wrong.

The two boys were standing just twenty feet in front of me. And they weren't running away.

I thought that was weird, but just wait. It gets weirder.

They pulled two large *hang gliders* out of the bushes. "Good thing we stashed these here. Huh, Fred?" said Jim.

"Shut up and jump."

"You first."

"No, you."

"No, *you*."

"Stupid."

"*You're* stupid."

I couldn't take it anymore. "You're *both* stupid!" I yelled.

The blond one looked at me. Then he grabbed his hang glider and started running to the edge of the cliff.

"Oh, no, you don't," I said. "You're not getting away this time."

Running and diving, I slammed against Jim's chest and wrapped my arms around his waist. The hang glider wobbled back and forth as we teetered toward the cliff.

"Let go!" Jim screamed.

"No way!" I screamed back.

We both went hurtling over the edge.

16.
Crash or Splash

By the time I reached the top of Pinewood Peak, it was too late.

"Joe! No!"

I watched in horror as the hang glider plunged over the side of the cliff. It was like seeing a movie in slow motion—and I couldn't do a thing to stop it. Joe was clinging on to Jim's waist, Jim was fumbling with the crossbar, and both of them were shrieking at the top of their lungs.

"*AAAUUUggghhhhhhhhhh!*"

Their screams faded as they fell. The glider jerked forward and plummeted downward. Then it disappeared from view.

Joe.

I ran to the edge of the cliff and looked down. It

didn't take me long to spot them. The large triangular sail of the glider was fluttering straight toward the rocks below.

They're done for, I thought.

But then something incredible happened.

The glider swooped upward. The warm night breeze filled the sail and lifted the glider up and away. Soaring over the lake like a hovering bird, it drifted across the moonlit sky and carried the two away.

I breathed a sigh of relief.

"Hey, Hardy! Get out of the way!"

I spun around and saw Fred, my dark-haired double, holding another hang glider. He leaned forward and came charging toward me like an angry bull, heading straight for the cliff.

"Up, up, and away!" he hollered, raising the sail.

He took a flying leap over the edge.

And I took a flying leap at *him.*

Wham!

I slammed against him with full force and held on tight. The impact sent the glider reeling and spinning out of control. As we plummeted downward, I had a sinking feeling that Fred and I were in big trouble.

But it worked for Joe and Jim.

The glider dipped and dropped faster and faster— like a lead balloon, as they say.

We're going to crash.

I closed my eyes. Fred started screaming. Then I

opened my eyes again—and saw the jagged rocks below. I started screaming too.

"*AAAAAAUUUUGGGGHHHH!*"

Fred and I kicked and swung our feet forward. The sail tilted and swerved upward and—*whoosh*—the glider swooped toward the lake. We missed hitting a big boulder by just a few feet.

We did it. We're flying!

We sailed in a long sweeping arc toward the lake. The large sail fluttered over our heads, pulling us upward. The force of it almost made me lose my grip around Fred's chest.

Letting go is not an option, I reminded myself.

Up, up, up, the hang glider rose slowly in the sky. My feet brushed against the tops of trees as we sailed higher and higher. Soon there was nothing below us but the calm water of Lake Midnight.

"Okay, Hardy. No free rides," Fred snarled. "Let go of me. *Now*."

"You've got to be kidding," I said, glancing down at the water hundreds of feet below.

"Do I sound like I'm kidding?" He twisted his whole body back and forth, trying to shake me off.

I tightened my grip. "Sorry, pal. But I think I'll just stick around for a while and enjoy the view."

Fred kicked me in the shins. "Come on! Let go! We're too heavy! We're losing altitude!"

He was right.

The hang glider was dropping faster by the minute. We definitely weren't going to make it to the other side of the lake—not at this rate.

I looked in the distance and saw Joe and Jim's glider, silhouetted in the moonlight.

Same thing.

It circled and dipped in a wide downward spiral over the center of the lake.

We're all going down, I thought.

Suddenly our sail rippled over our heads. Then it went slack. The whole glider jerked—and we started plunging down toward the water.

"Get off, Hardy! You're messing it up!"

"That's right," I shouted. "And I'm taking you with me!"

Down, down, down, the glider twirled and whirled in a wild, crazy freefall. Fred and I leaned hard on the crossbar, trying to gain control of the fluttering sail. We veered to the right, then to the left, and all of a sudden . . .

"Look out!" I yelled.

We crashed into Joe and Jim's hang glider.

CRUNCH!

It came out of nowhere, swooping down on us in its rapid descent. The two gliders buckled from the blow. The frames of the sails bent and everything just collapsed.

Fred and I screamed. Joe and Jim screamed. And then down we went.

It's all over now. We're going to get wet.

Taking a deep breath, I prepared myself for the impact.

SPLASH!

SPLASH!

One after the other, the hang gliders plunged into the water. It was like being slapped really hard by a giant, cold hand. I had no idea how deep we plummeted, but it must have been ten or fifteen feet below the surface. With the hang glider sinking down on top of me, it felt like I was trapped at the bottom of the ocean.

I tried to stay calm. Letting go of Fred, I kicked my feet and attempted to swim.

Wham!

Something banged against my jaw. I think it was Fred's foot, but I couldn't be sure. I couldn't see a thing.

Which way is up?

Maybe I was a little stunned, but I couldn't get my bearings. I spun around, felt the broken sail of the glider, and looked around.

The moon.

The light gleamed through the water above me, beckoning me to the surface. Moving my arms in long, steady strokes, I kicked my feet hard and jettisoned upward.

Air!

I came up gasping and shaking. Turning my head from side to side, I looked for the others. A second later a few bubbles broke the surface—and someone emerged from the deep.

"Joe! You made it!"

"Of course I made it." My brother blinked his eyes and pushed his hair back. "What happened to the terrible twosome?"

"I don't know."

They were nowhere to be seen. The lake rippled softly in the moonlight, and I started to wonder if Fred and Jim were still trapped under their gliders—and sinking to the bottom.

"Frank! Over there!"

Joe pointed across the lake. I squinted my eyes and noticed two figures splashing around in the moonlight.

It was Fred and Jim.

They were at least fifty feet away from us—and swimming straight toward the docks. *How had they gotten so far ahead?*

"Come on!" said Joe, swimming after them.

I followed right behind him, stroking and paddling as fast as I could. Our opponents had a pretty big lead, but I wasn't worried about it. Not to sound conceited, but Joe and I are champion swimmers. And we have a wall full of medals back home to prove it.

Yeah, so they were from summer kiddie camp. So what.

In a matter of minutes, Joe and I caught up with them. I went after Fred, and Joe went after Jim. Swimming up from behind, we just reached out and grabbed them.

They never saw us coming.

"Hey!"

"You . . . *grggle, grggle.*"

Fred's head slipped under the water before he finished his sentence. He held on tight as he kicked and struggled beneath me.

Then, without warning, he came up fighting.

Pow!

His fist slammed hard against my jaw.

Splash!

I reeled back, my head spinning.

And then I started to sink.

For a moment there, I thought I was going to drown. My whole body went limp, and cold water filled my mouth. But then I started to revive, shaking myself awake and rising to the surface.

When I reached the top, Fred was gone. I looked toward the docks and spotted him, swimming toward the shore.

Give it up, Fred. I'm a faster swimmer.

Before I took off after him, I glanced over at Joe and Jim. They thrashed next to me in the water, pushing and pulling, kicking and swinging, bobbing up and down as they fought.

Just imagine championship wrestling in a giant pool.

You get the idea.

Get him, Joe.

I was tempted to help my brother out, but I knew he could handle the guy by himself.

And anyway, I had my own evil twin to worry about.

I turned toward the shore and looked for Fred. He was already halfway to the docks, and I knew I'd have to swim like crazy to catch up. So I kicked my feet and started swimming like a maniac, my arms beating the water with fast, steady strokes.

Faster, faster . . . move it!

I used the same technique that helped me win more than a few high school swim meets.

But this time, there was more than a shiny medal at stake.

Faster, faster . . .

The water splashed across my face with every breath I took. As I turned my head, I thought I heard something—even with the water in my ears.

I listened again.

What's that?

The sound came from the docks. It sounded like the motor of a boat.

I stopped swimming and looked over.

Jake.

The burly ex-convict sat at the controls of a white speedboat tied to the docks. I saw him wave at his son in the water. Then he revved up the engine, untied the rope, and pushed off.

Zzzzzzzoooom!

The speedboat took off like a bullet, shooting across the lake and swerving around in a large circle. The rippling waves made me bob up and down in the water. I looked back at Joe and Jim. They had stopped fighting to see what was happening. Then Jim started swimming away. Fast. *Huh?*

Zzzzzzzoooom!

The speedboat veered and turned, setting a course back to the shore. Jake gunned the engine a few times, then headed toward us.

I figured he was planning to help his boys out of the water.

But I was wrong.

Instead he spun the boat around and pointed it right at *me*. Then he kicked it into high gear. The speedboat blazed across the water, moving faster and faster, closer and closer.

I tried to swim out of the way, but it was too late.

The speedboat was going to hit me, and there was nothing I could do about it.

This is it, I thought. *I'm fish food.*

17.
The Need for Speed

"Dive, Frank! Dive!"

I knew my brother couldn't hear me over the noise of the speedboat—but I couldn't just watch him get mowed over without at least trying.

Whoosh!

The boat zoomed across the water, aiming for his head.

Swoosh!

Frank ducked down—just in the nick of time. The boat glided right over him.

He's okay, I thought.

If Jake had actually hit him, I would have heard some kind of loud *thump*. So Frank must have dropped deep enough to miss the hull of the boat.

I let out a sigh of relief and waited for my brother's head to pop out of the water.

Okay. Where are you, Frank?

I waited a few more seconds. Nothing happened. He didn't come up for air. Then I started to worry.

What about the propeller? Maybe it hit him. Maybe he's bleeding.

I held my breath.

Maybe he's drowning.

My worries disappeared when Frank shot up out of the water, gasping and waving. I started to wave back. But then I realized that something was wrong.

Frank wasn't waving. He was pointing.

I turned my head—and ducked.

Zzzzzzzooooommmm!

Jake's speedboat barreled over me, grazing my shoulder and spinning me around in the water. I floundered for a few moments in the churning wave before coming up for air.

Man! That was close!

But it wasn't over yet. Jake had turned the boat around for another go at me.

Zzzzzzzooooommmm!

This time I was ready for it. I was able to dive down before the speedboat reached me, going just deep enough to avoid a collision.

But I felt the force of the propeller.

The whirling blades ripped past my head so quickly that I was lucky I didn't lose an ear.

Yikes.

Holding my breath, I glided along beneath the surface

of the lake. I tried to get as far away from my original position as I could—so Jake wouldn't use me as a human boat ramp.

Finally I had to come up for air. I gazed up at the surface, making sure it was calm. I listened for the sound of an approaching speedboat. Nothing. So I slowly raised my head in the water.

Where did everybody go?

It took me a second to realize that I'd swum to the center of the lake. Frank and the docks were far behind me. Turning around, I squinted my eyes and quickly scanned the shoreline.

There's Jake. But what's he doing? Why did he stop the boat?

About fifty feet away from the docks, the speedboat floated along gently, its motor idling. Jake leaned over the side and pulled something out of the water. I had to wipe the water from my eyes before I realized what it was.

Jim.

His blond dyed hair hung down over his face, wet and limp. He looked like a drowned rat—with a bad hairstyle. He was sputtering and pointing toward us.

Suddenly I saw something move in the water, just a few yards away from the boat.

Frank?

No. It was Fred, who didn't look much better than his drowned-rat brother. I could tell by the slow way he was swimming that Fred was totally exhausted. It took all hands on deck to drag his tired butt out of the water and into the boat.

So where's Frank? I wondered.

I didn't have to wait long to find out—because Fred pointed right at him. My brother was about a hundred feet away, swimming to shore.

Jake revved up the motor for another attack. His sons cheered—and braced themselves. Then, gunning the engine, Jake steered toward his target and blasted across the lake.

Look out, Frank. Here they come.

The speedboat circled around him like a great white shark.

Then it moved in for the kill.

Zzzzzzooooommmmm!

Frank ducked down and disappeared. The boat veered around, preparing for another attack. The second my brother came up for air, he had to dive right down again.

Zzzzzzooooommmmm!

Jake was relentless, swinging the boat around again and again.

The guy won't give up, I thought.

But neither would Frank.

My brother could keep it up all night if he had to. And from the looks of things, Jake was going to keep it up all night too.

I have to do something, I thought. *Anything.*

Swimming as fast as I could, I headed for the boathouse on the edge of the lake. There were a bunch of speedboats tied to the dock, and maybe—just maybe—somebody had left their key in the ignition.

Fat chance, I thought.

But hey, it was the only chance I had.

Jake and his sons kept driving the speedboat back and forth, playing cat and mouse with my brother. They didn't even notice me climbing up onto one of the docks. I ducked down and crept along silently, moving swiftly from one empty boat to the other.

No key, no key, no . . . *wait.*

I stopped in my tracks.

Yes!

I couldn't believe my luck, but there it was—a speedboat with its key in the ignition. I hopped inside, untied the boat from the dock, and sat down at the wheel. I kept my fingers crossed as I turned the key.

The speedboat roared to life.

Yes!

I didn't waste any time. Steering away from the dock, I shifted into high gear and zoomed across the lake. Staying close to the shoreline, I headed straight toward Jake and his sons—who were still racing back and forth, trying to hit Frank.

Keep it up, jerks. I'm going to blow you right out of the water.

I raced up beside them while they were making a

turn. They didn't see me until it was too late.

CRUNCH!

I plowed into the back of their boat and spun them around and around.

At first Jake and his sons just stared at me in silent shock. Then they started shouting and shaking their fists.

"What do you think you're doing?"

"You're dead, Hardy!"

"Get him, boys!"

Fred and Jim stood up and tried to climb onto my boat—but I sped away before they got the chance. Veering to the left, I circled back to Frank, who was treading water and watching the whole thing.

I zoomed up next to him and stopped.

"Hi, Frank. Need a lift?"

"Sure. Why not?"

Reaching up, he grabbed the edge of the speedboat and hoisted himself out of the water. Then, flopping down next to me, he closed his eyes and let out a huge sigh.

"What's wrong, Frank?" I asked. "You look a little tired."

He opened his eyes and gave me a dirty look.

"You should try aerobics," I went on, "to increase your stamina."

"Um, Joe . . ."

"Or maybe one of those dance workout videos they advertise on TV."

"Joe . . ."

"Or maybe a yoga class."

"Joe!"

"What, Frank?"

"Are you planning to do anything about the speedboat that's about to hit us?"

I looked up—and gasped.

Jake's boat was just fifty feet away and heading toward us at about fifty miles an hour.

You do the math.

Zzzzzzooooommmmm!

I grabbed the accelerator and spun the wheel, just barely avoiding a head-on collision. Speeding away to the center of the lake, I turned the boat around and glanced back at Jake and his sons.

Their speedboat was a few hundred feet away. Pivoting slowly, and aiming straight for us, it came to a complete stop.

Then Jake started revving the engine.

"Check it out," I said. "They want to play chicken."

My brother groaned. "Chicken? Again? You know I hate this game, Joe."

"Aw, come on. It'll be fun."

"You said that the last time we played chicken."

"So?"

"So you ended up flipping over a dune buggy!"

"So?"

"So we could have been killed!"

162

"Get over it, Frank. We're going to play chicken," I said, "because we don't have a choice."

I pointed across the lake. Jake's boat was racing toward us, skimming over the water and picking up speed. I grabbed the wheel of our boat, revved the motor, and let it fly.

Okay, Jake. Bring it on.

Faster and faster, closer and closer, our speedboats sliced a matching pair of white foaming paths across the moonlit surface of Lake Midnight. Waves rippled. Motors roared.

If neither boat swerved away, we were definitely going to crash. And crash hard.

"Slow down, Joe!"

"No!"

Frank knew it was useless to argue at this point. So he sat back and braced himself.

Zzzzzzooooommmmmm!

We were close enough now that I could see the faces of everyone in the other boat. Jake gritted his teeth and laughed like a lunatic. Fred threw his head back and howled. And Jim—*what a weirdo*—bobbed up and down in his seat like a broken crazy-haired jack-in-the-box.

The speedboats rocketed toward each other, just fifty feet apart. Forty feet, thirty feet, twenty feet . . .

"Turn, Joe! Turn!"

I ignored my brother and waited for the right moment.

Ten feet, five . . .

"Joe! Look out!"

At the very last second, I pulled on the wheel and veered to the right.

SCRRRRUNCH!

The two boats careened off each other at full speed. The sides scraped together as we passed, rocking both boats and almost knocking me out of my seat.

That's when I got the surprise of my life.

Jim—my crazy-haired evil twin—jumped up and swung a plastic oar at my face.

Pow!

I flew backward into the boat, reeling from the blow.

That stupid jack-in-the-box!

Then I blacked out.

18.
Rock and Roll

Joe went down so fast I didn't have time to get out of the way.

Whump!

Direct hit.

He landed right on top of me, pinning me down on the floor of the boat.

"Joe? Are you okay? Joe?"

No response.

I tried to push him off, but he wouldn't budge. I don't know why. Maybe his belt loop was snagged on something or Jim's oar was wedged over his chest.

All I know is this: His foot was wedged against the controls. The accelerator was stuck.

The boat roared along at top speed, skipping and bouncing over the waves. The motion made me feel sick. I thought I was going to throw up.

Then I thought of something important.

Nobody's steering.

The speedboat raced forward—blindly—and all I could do was lay there and look up at the moon.

"Joe! Wake up! Joe!"

My brother let out a little groan and shifted his body a few inches—just enough for me to squeeze my way out from beneath him. Sitting up and raising my head, I looked over the steering wheel.

Oh, man! Give me a break!

We were heading straight for one of the docks.

And judging from the speed we were moving, we would crash in about fifteen seconds.

I glanced down at the controls. Joe's foot was twisted against the accelerator. I didn't have time to move it, so I grabbed the wheel and spun it as hard as I could.

Whooooosh!

The boat veered to the side, creating a mini tidal wave that crashed against the docks. Arcing to the left, we drew closer and closer to one of the large wooden posts at the water's edge.

I wasn't sure we were going to make it. So I pulled the wheel another inch to the left.

Swooosh!

The speedboat tilted and swerved—and just missed the dock.

Water sprayed and splashed all around us. I tried to straighten the wheel and maintain a steady course. But the sheer speed of the boat—and the fact that I was sitting on Joe's leg—made it hard to control.

"Joe! Wake up!"

My brother groaned and shifted again. But he didn't take his foot off the controls.

I looked up again—and gasped.

Without even trying, I had somehow managed to zoom up behind Jake and his sons. Their speedboat was right in front of us. They were trying to get away but didn't seem to have quite as much power.

In fact, if they didn't speed up soon, we were going to crash into the back of their boat.

Move it, Jake.

I had no choice. I had to turn the wheel and veer to the side. But I didn't realize how close we were to the docks. There wasn't enough room to make a full turn. No matter which way I steered, I was going to hit something.

"Frank? What's going on?"

Finally—my brother was waking up.

"Joe! Lift your foot! Hurry!"

He bolted upright, moved his foot, and grabbed the controls with his hands. The boat slowed down almost instantly. I was able to turn and reposition ourselves so we were right behind Jake and his sons again.

I settled into the driver's seat and followed them all the way to the far end of the lake.

"That's weird," I said to Joe. "Why aren't they turning

around? If they keep going straight, they're going to hit the river."

"Maybe it's part of their getaway plan."

"No. The river's too shallow and rocky for boats. They wouldn't get very far. Unless . . ."

"Unless what?"

"Unless they're too stupid to know that," I finished.

Joe laughed. "Are you kidding? Those guys are *mega super* stupid."

I slowed down as we approached the small river that drained from the end of the lake. Jake and his sons were slowing down too—but they weren't stopping.

"Look! They're doing it," I said. "They're turning onto the river. I can't believe it."

"Believe it," said Joe. "But think of it, Frank. It'll be easy to catch them once their boat is dragging on the bottom."

I turned and looked my brother in the eye. "So you think we should follow them?"

"I think we should follow them. What's the worst that could happen?"

I sighed. "We could wreck another vehicle that doesn't belong to us."

Joe shrugged. "I'm willing to risk it."

"Why am I not surprised?"

It was settled. We were going after the bad guys—once again. But just as we were about to turn off and head down the river, we heard police sirens on the other side of the lake. Looking back, we saw our cabin surrounded by a bunch of squad cars with their lights flashing.

"Well, it looks like Officer Stern got his backup," I said. "Finally."

Joe sighed. "Yeah, I suppose we should go back and tell the police where to find Jake and his goon squad."

He gave me a sad puppy-dog look, then waited for my reply.

"Nah," I said. "That would be too easy. If you want something done right, Joe, you've got to do it yourself. And besides, *it'll be fun*."

My brother broke out smiling. "You're the *man*, Frank!"

"No, *you're* the man, Joe!"

"Let's rock and roll!"

I gunned the speedboat's engine, grabbed the controls, and set off down the river. The branches of the trees hanging over the water made it harder to see. The dappled moonlight looked like tiny rocks sprinkled in our path—and I started to worry about the *actual* rocks waiting ahead.

"Faster, Frank. We need to catch up."

"Don't worry. Once they hit the shallow part, they won't be going anywhere."

I expected our boat to scrape against the bottom at any moment—but it never happened. In fact, the whole river seemed deeper than I remembered.

It was faster, too.

And wilder.

Soon the current was carrying us along at a swift and steady clip. Then it started getting rougher. We rocked from side to side, rising and falling as the water rolled across the rocks.

"I've never gone white-water rafting in a speedboat before," I said.

"Well, Frank, it looks like you're about to get a crash course."

"Let's hope not."

I held the wheel with both hands. Joe leaned back and shifted his weight to help navigate the ups and downs. Between the two of us, we managed to keep pretty high and dry.

But all that changed when we hit the rapids.

"Hold on!" I yelled.

Whoosh!

The speedboat jerked downward, water splashing over the sides. Then it teetered back again, and I thought the whole thing was going to flip over.

"Frank! Look out for the rock!"

The current slammed the boat forward, and we careened toward a large boulder. I had to reach up and brace my arm against the rock to keep the boat upright. The back end swung around, and soon we were spinning out of control, completely at the mercy of the raging river.

We'll never make it, I thought.

But after a few more dips and bobs, the water started getting calmer. After a minute or two, I was able to gain control of the boat and guide us safely down the river.

At one point the moon disappeared behind a cloud—and I could barely see where I was going. "We'll never find them if that cloud doesn't move," I said.

"Do you still have the night-vision goggles?"

I shook my head. "I must have dropped my backpack somewhere. Probably when I was climbing Pinewood Peak."

"Or hang gliding over the cliff."

"Or dive-bombing into the lake."

"Or dodging the speedboat."

We laughed.

Suddenly the cloud drifted away from the moon, and the river glowed in the silver light.

"Frank! There they are!"

I looked up and spotted the infamous white speedboat. Jake, Fred, and Jim didn't look like they were in much of a hurry—until they glanced back and saw us.

"Dad! It's them!" shouted one of the boys.

"Stupid Hardys," grumbled the other.

Jake hit the accelerator. The speedboat lurched forward, picking up speed as it rounded the bend of the river. But Joe and I were right behind them.

"Keep it up, Frank! We're gaining on them!"

The river twisted and turned—and the two boats twisted and turned right along with it. I zoomed closer and tried to force Jake's boat over to the river's edge.

BAM!

I hit a rock.

BAM! BAM!

I hit two rocks.

Suddenly we were in the middle of white-water rapids, banging against the rocks like a couple of steel balls in a pinball machine. It wasn't as bad as before—but it was bad enough to do some damage.

CRUNCH!

A huge, jagged rock ripped a big hole in the side of our speedboat. Water gushed over the sides, dousing our feet and legs. Joe started bailing it out with his hands, but I knew it was a waste of time.

Our boat was sinking. Fast.

Hopefully it would hold together just long enough to carry us to the calmer waters ahead. I looked up to see how Jake and his crew were faring. They were out of the rapids and heading toward a small bridge.

"Joe! Look!"

I pointed to a parked car on the bridge. A tall man jumped out and ran to the edge of the river. Hopping from rock to rock, he made his way toward the middle, then crouched down on a large, flat boulder.

"Frank! Look who it is!"

Dad! He must have seen our speedboats take off down the river, then jumped in his car to intercept us.

He waited for the speedboat to get a little closer to the edge, then he sprang up, leaped onto the boat, and dove on top of Jake.

WHUMP!

They smashed against the sides, falling backward and flipping overboard.

SPLASH!

The two men hit the water—and came up swinging. Jake grabbed my father's head and tried to shove him under. But a couple of right hooks from Dad sent the bigger man reeling.

"Get him!" I shouted.

Joe and I were so swept up in the fight that we almost forgot about Fred and Jim. Somehow the two boys had managed to turn their speedboat around. By the time we saw them coming toward us, it was too late.

"Frank!"

The boat zoomed across the river at a speed that wasn't just dangerous—it was downright crazy. Jim was at the wheel, his dyed blond hair as wild and wacky as the gleam in his eye.

I hit the accelerator and tried to get out of the way. But no such luck. Our boat was flooded.

We were totally sunk.

The white speedboat rocketed toward us.

Then—with a loud *CRUNCH*—it smashed against a rock, flew up into the air, and came down on top of us.

POLICE BULLETIN

June 15, 1:00 a.m.
SUSPECTS ESCAPING IN SPEEDBOATS

ATTENTION: all patrol cars. Three suspects, a large man and two teenage boys, have fled the scene of a crime at Lake Midnight. After holding several people captive inside a cabin, the culprits managed to escape on foot. They were last seen driving a white speedboat across the lake and are now heading down the river.

Please post all available officers along various points on the river, especially Brimstone Bridge near the rapids. It's the last place a boat could stay afloat before hitting Rockwater Falls. If they go over the falls, they'll never survive.

Also: The suspects are not to be confused with Frank and Joe Hardy, the teenagers who were originally thought to be involved in a series of robberies and holdups. The Hardys are innocent.

Repeat: The Hardys are innocent.

Over and out.

19.
Overboard

Okay, so I was sitting there with my brother in a sinking boat, watching my Dad slug it out with a major mental case, and our evil twins came flying down from the sky to flatten us with a speedboat.

Here's how I handled the situation.

First I looked up and thought, *So that's what the bottom of a speedboat looks like.*

And then I thought, *So this is how I'm going to die.*

I certainly wasn't thrilled about it. The bottom of a speedboat is nothing special. And being squashed like a bug by two losers with bad attitudes and bad hair is no way to die.

Sorry, man, not tonight.

So Frank and I did what anyone would do. We jumped off that little sinking ship as fast as humanly possible—just a split second before it was totally flattened.

CRRRUNCH!

The flying speedboat slammed down hard and heavy. The sheer force of it almost blew Frank and me right out of the water. Our boat was smashed to bits. The pieces that didn't sink to the bottom were sliced and diced by the motor's propeller blades.

Fred and Jim veered off toward the river's edge. Then they spun around to survey the damage.

"We got 'em, Fred!"

"Yeah, we totally flattened 'em! Like pancakes!"

Frank and I swam behind a river rock and hid ourselves.

They think we're dead.

Fred nudged his brother. "It's kind of weird, isn't it?"

"What's weird?"

"Them being dead. They were all Dad ever talked about. 'Frank and Joe, Frank and Joe. You got to get revenge against Frank and Joe.' And now what?"

"They're dead," said Jim.

"Yeah. So you can stop dying your hair now."

"I don't know. I kind of like being a blond."

"Shut up, stupid."

"*You're* stupid."

Frank and I ducked down to stifle our laughs.

When we looked back, Fred had turned the boat around to face downriver. "Check it out. Dad's going to massacre that Hardy guy."

I glanced at Frank, then cast my eyes toward the bridge.

Dad and Jake were still going at it. But now they were fighting on the bank of the river. I started to get a little worried when I saw Jake tackle our father to the ground. But then the two of them rolled into the shallow water, and Dad was on top.

Fred and Jim hooted and whistled as if they were watching a celebrity slugfest on pay-per-view TV.

My brother nudged me and nodded toward the speedboat. "Come on, Joe," he whispered. "Let's take care of these mental midgets."

"What about Dad?"

Frank glanced back at the riverbank. Our father rolled Jake onto his stomach and pulled his arm behind his back until the big guy screamed.

"I think Dad's going to be okay," said Frank.

I had to agree.

Taking a deep breath and ducking down, we glided toward the speedboat like a pair of crocodiles. Then we braced our feet on some rocks—and prepared to attack.

Fred and Jim never saw it coming.

First we jumped out of the water and into the boat.

Then we introduced ourselves.

"Hi, Fred," said Frank. "I'm your worst nightmare."

The dark-haired boy looked up in shock.

"Hi, Jim," I said to the other. "I'm your not-so-evil twin."

The two of them stared at us as if they were seeing ghosts. But then it hit me.

They think we're dead.

I'm sure they realized the truth when we jumped on top of them and started fighting.

WHUMP!

The four of us landed in a jumbled heap on the bottom of the boat. Arms and legs and fists were flying. Jim tried punching me in the face a few times, but I managed to block his blows. And Fred started to strangle Frank but lost his grip when my brother socked him on the chin.

POW!

Jim jumped to his feet. I scrambled after him, catching his ankle before he could crawl out of the boat. I pulled hard and . . .

WHAM!

He landed with a thud against the boat's control panel.

It took me a second or two to realize that the motor was churning and the speedboat was moving. I tried to pull Jim away from the controls. He bent his knee and planted his foot against my chest, then kicked me away with a hard shove.

I staggered back and almost fell off the boat.

That's when I noticed we were under the bridge and barreling downriver.

I glanced back and caught one last glimpse of Dad and Jake on the riverbank.

Get him, Dad. You can take him.

Then I noticed flashing red lights up on the bridge. Two squad cars pulled up, and cops started getting out and heading over to Dad and Jake. They grabbed Jake and cuffed him, while some rescue workers hurried to Dad's side.

Phew.

With that over, I turned back to face my personal demon—a bleached-blond dunce named Jim.

"Bring it on, Hardy," he sneered at me.

He leaned back against the controls, pushing the accelerator until we were zooming full speed down the river. I took a deep breath and leaped on top of him.

BAM!

We both went down—crashing hard against Frank and Fred. The speedboat rocked back and forth and up and down.

From this point on, it was all-out war.

You want me to bring it on? I'll bring it on.

Kicking, shoving, jabbing, punching—it was hard to tell who was who and what was what. But our diabolical doubles just wouldn't give up, and neither would we.

Even when the speedboat hit a rock.

CRRRRUUUNCH!

It ripped a huge hole in the side of the boat. Water started pouring in, and the whole thing started to sink. Fast.

Going, going, gone.

We plunged into the cold water, still locked in combat. Bobbing up and down, we clung to our enemies and tried to stay afloat. But the current was incredibly strong. We kept dunking down and grazing against rocks, only to be swept up again and carried along.

"Your dad's a squealer!" Jim shouted in my ear. "A dirty rotten squealer!"

"*Your* dad's a lunatic!" I shouted back. "And your dye job stinks!"

He slammed his fist against my head so hard that my ears were ringing. At least that's what I thought at first.

What's that sound?

I raised my head above the water and tried to listen. Something in the distance was rumbling and roaring.

Suddenly it hit me.

Rockwater Falls.

We were heading right for them!

I glanced at the riverbanks to see if I could spot any kind of landmark that might tell me how close we were to the falls. But it wasn't necessary. When I looked downstream, I could see the river ahead of us—plunging over the edge.

"Frank! Frank!"

I started yelling my brother's name as loud as I could. I glanced over at him as he struggled in the bubbling foam with Fred.

"Frank!"

He looked over his shoulder and saw me. Then I waved and pointed toward the falls. He seemed to understand—because he said something to Fred, and they both started swimming upstream, angling toward the shore.

"Jim! We have to get out! We're heading for the falls!"

The blond weirdo just looked at me and laughed.

He doesn't understand.

Or maybe he just didn't care. He was raised for revenge, after all. Maybe he was so brainwashed by his father that he would try to kill me even if it killed him.

I glanced back at Frank and Fred. The river shoved them straight toward a huge rock.

BAM!

They crashed right into it.

"AAAAUUUGGGHHH!"

Fred howled in pain. I watched as Frank climbed up onto the rock—and dragged Fred out of the water. There was blood all over Fred's leg. It looked like he'd broken it.

But at least Frank would take care of him until an emergency team arrived.

As for me, I was being squeezed to death by Jim—who wouldn't let me go no matter how hard I tried to fight him off. Suddenly the river started moving faster and faster. And we started moving closer and closer to the edge.

It's all over now, I thought. *We're going over the falls.*

We were about fifty feet away. I spotted a big rock jutting up along the edge. Kicking my feet really fast, I tried to set a course for the rock.

"Hey, Hardy!" Jim shouted. "Can't wait to see you fall!"

"Don't hold your breath!"

The water roared around us, and the current thrust us toward the edge.

WHAM!

We hit the rock dead-on. I started scrambling up—but Jim kept trying to pull me back. Finally he climbed up and threw himself on top of me. I was pinned down with my head hanging over the falls.

I could hear the water crashing onto the rocks hundreds of feet below.

"Die, Hardy! Die!"

Jim wrapped his hands around my neck and started squeezing. I kicked and squirmed beneath him and struggled to breathe. Finally I raised my right hand and . . .

POW!

I socked him in the face. Jim teetered back—and fell. I reached out and grabbed his wrist as he swung over the edge, dangling over the rushing water.

He looked up at me, his face filled with shock and horror. "Help," he said.

I sighed. "I should let you fall," I said. "But I won't. That's the difference between you and me. I'm one of the good guys."

Then I reached down with my other hand, grabbed ahold of his arm, and hauled him up to safety.

It took a little while for the emergency rescue team to get us off of there. They used a high-powered boat to save Frank and Fred. But for Jim and me, they had to drop a rescuer down from a helicopter.

It was pretty cool. After we were reunited with our dad, the police gave us a ride back to the cabin. Dad, Frank, and I talked about what had just happened— and tried to figure out how we were going to explain all our scrapes and bruises to Mom and Aunt Trudy. Even though they knew about our being framed, they couldn't know *all* the details—or they might never let us out of the house again.

"No problem," said Dad. "We'll just say we were playing extreme sports on a short fishing trip we took right after this case was closed. You know, to let off some steam. There's no reason they need to know about any of this chase business. Agreed?"

Frank and I agreed.

"Okay, then," he said. "Mum's the word."

HARDY HEROES CATCH LOOK-ALIKE CROOKS!

Former Cop's Sons Are Chips Off the Old Block

(*Bayport County News*)
Former police detective Fenton Hardy and his sons, Frank and Joe, thwarted the twisted revenge plot of ex-convict Jake Johansen last night. Johansen, a former police officer who was busted for robbery, theft, and criminal corruption, enlisted his own two sons, Frederick and James, to frame the Hardy brothers by impersonating them in a series of local crimes.

Full story inside.

Epilogue

It was the perfect day for a bank withdrawal.

The weatherman had predicted clear skies, and for once he was right. The sun was shining, and everyone in town was out and about, enjoying the beautiful day.

That meant fewer people indoors.

Perfect.

Two boys stood in the bank line, waiting for the teller to finish a transaction.

The younger blond teenager sighed. "Do we really have to take out *all* of our savings? I worked hard for that money."

His dark-haired brother nodded. "Just drop it. You know we have to pay for that boat we destroyed, not to mention the dirt bikes and dune buggy we 'borrowed' at the Vehicle Park. It's the law."

"What makes you so sure?"

"I'm the smart one, remember?"

The teller behind the window looked up at the two boys. She had curly red hair, thick glasses—and a puzzled look on her face. "Um, can I help you boys?" she asked.

The dark-haired teen reached into his pocket and

pulled out two withdrawal slips. "We'd like to withdraw all our money from our accounts, please."

The teller glanced down at the slips. "Oh, my," she muttered. Her mouth dropped open, and her eyes nearly popped out of her head.

The boys expected a reaction like this.

Ever since that newspaper story, people seemed to recognize them everywhere they went.

They were "heroes" now, or so the paper claimed.

The teller bit her lip and started counting out their money. She stuffed the cash into two small envelopes and slipped them through the slot in the window.

The older boy took them and smiled. "Thanks, ma'am," he said. "It was nice doing business with you."

The two boys turned and walked past the sleeping guard.

The older boy looked at his brother. "Come on," he said. "Let's get out of here, Joe."

"I'm right behind you, Frank."

And the two boys ran out of the bank and into the sunlight.